Praise for *Th*

"Beyond the novel's taut suspense and subtle characterization, Pitlor's vivid prose provides an additional pleasure . . . The novel's suspense lasts right until its shocking climax, but the 'messy, wonderful, excruciating lives' of its characters linger in the mind long after the last page." —*The Boston Globe*

"The mystery will keep you on the edge of your beach chair, but the real attraction to this book is the author's beautiful portrayal of a marriage in peril, of two people whose lives have become heartbreakingly ordinary, and how it forever altered their personalities." —*Coastal Living*

"Pitlor brings forth the emotions that surge beneath the surface with the precision and power of a conductor . . . This powerful analysis of how dreams become nightmares will make readers want to hold their loved ones close."

—*Booklist,* starred review

"The novel's easy blending of crime and family narrative deftly cracks open the closed world of Lovell and Hannah's marriage. In this exploration of a woman lost, and a lost love, Pitlor exposes every secret—frustrations, weaknesses, ugliness—to the harsh light of day." —*Toronto Star*

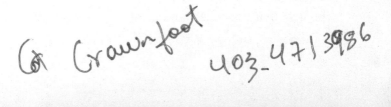

"A perfect microscope with which to examine the inexhaustible fascinations of marriage, and as Pitlor flashes between the day of Hannah's disappearance and Lovell's uneasy consideration of their past resentments, she finds a nice voice—thoughtful, lyrical, unforced."

—*The New York Times Book Review*

"This Stephen King–approved 'hypnotically readable' novel involves a wife who's vanished and a husband who's trying to understand what's happened, but it's not just another *Gone Girl*."

—*Health Magazine*

"[H]eartbreaking and heart stopping, and kept me up late into the night."

—KMUW, Wichita Public Radio

"Pitlor ramps up the suspense in this story of a marriage gone sour and a wife who has vanished . . . A riveting and distinctive first novel."

—BBC.com

"The strength of *The Daylight Marriage* lies in its structure, coupled with a clear, piercing cadence in each sentence."

—*Los Angeles Review of Books*

"Despite the acrid marriage, the his-and-hers narration, and the fact that Lovell quickly emerges as the primary suspect, this isn't really another *Gone Girl*. It's more an exploration of the way that the tiniest and most impetuous of decisions can suddenly recast a person's life."

—*Entertainment Weekly*

"This is a classic page-turner with just the right amount of human story behind it. The narrative Pitlor constructs for us is a harrowing and deeply real tale of loss: loss of innocence, of loved ones, of ourselves." —EverydayEbook.com

"*The Daylight Marriage* may not be a mystery novel in the classical sense, but the incremental revelations create a similar momentum . . . It's fascinating to watch Pitlor test and prod female archetypes." —*Harvard Review*

"This spellbinding novel of suspense from the author of *The Birthdays* is told with great sympathy, as tension builds toward an inexorable conclusion. It can also be read as a cautionary tale both about a failed marriage and about how one impulsive decision can lead to a very dark place." —*Library Journal*

"In *The Daylight Marriage* there are two mysteries—the whereabouts of a missing woman and the vagaries of the human heart. Heidi Pitlor explores both of these enigmas with equal mastery. Pitlor merges a shocking crime story with an incisive portrait of a failed marriage. The result is a novel that is fast-moving, emotionally complex, and ultimately heartbreaking."
—Tom Perrotta, author of *Nine Inches*

THE DAYLIGHT MARRIAGE

ALSO BY HEIDI PITLOR
The Birthdays

THE
DAYLIGHT
MARRIAGE

~ A NOVEL ~

Heidi Pitlor

ALGONQUIN BOOKS
OF CHAPEL HILL
2016

Published by
ALGONQUIN BOOKS OF CHAPEL HILL
Post Office Box 2225
Chapel Hill, North Carolina 27515-2225

a division of
WORKMAN PUBLISHING
225 Varick Street
New York, New York 10014

First paperback edition, Algonquin Books of Chapel Hill,
January 2016. Originally published in hardcover by Algonquin
Books of Chapel Hill, May 2015.
Printed in the United States of America.
Published simultaneously in Canada by Thomas Allen & Son Limited.
Design by Anne Winslow.

This is a work of fiction. While, as in all fiction, the literary
perceptions and insights are based on experience, all names,
characters, places, and incidents either are products of the
author's imagination or are used fictitiously.

LIBRARY OF CONGRESS CATALOGING-IN-PUBLICATION DATA
Pitlor, Heidi.
The daylight marriage : a novel / by Heidi Pitlor.—First edition.
pages ; cm
ISBN 978-1-61620-368-9 (HC)
I. Title.
PS3616.I875D39 2015
813'.6—dc23

2014042713

ISBN 978-1-61620-531-7 (PB)

10 9 8 7 6 5 4 3 2 1
First Paperback Edition

For my father, Joel Ross Pitlor

Home is so far from Home.

—EMILY DICKINSON

↝

Life itself may be part of
the answer to the riddle
of the faint young sun.

—KERRY EMANUEL,
What We Know about Climate Change

Chapter 1

Later, in weaker moments, Lovell Hall reminded himself of the logical fallacy that young scientists so often committed: *Post hoc, ergo propter hoc.* After this, therefore because of this. Of course, without certain information—and in the face of other unfortunate realities—the timing of that evening with his wife was impossible to ignore.

On the way home from his office in Cambridge, he had come to a stop in traffic with little more to look at than the back end of a maroon Dodge minivan and the rusted undercarriage of a semi. He was hungry. He was dizzy with hunger. This was the wrong day to have skipped lunch; he would probably miss dinner with his family again. And he had vowed to Hannah to make it home in time, for once. He had even left Mass Environmental before five. But because the universe had a way of conspiring against him, specifically when it came to being the husband that Hannah wanted, here he was with his car idling on high, here he sat mumbling obscenities about the minivan and the other commuters who drove instead of taking the train (his own office was nowhere near a train station), anticipating her barely muffled wrath when he got home.

When he finally opened the front door of his house an hour and a half after he had left Cambridge, he dropped his jacket at the foot of the stairs and went toward the kitchen. "I'm ravenous," he said to Hannah as he helped himself to the soupy dregs of spaghetti at the bottom of the bowl. The two kids cleared their plates. She rose to collect the other dishes and glasses around him on the table.

"Route Two was a parking lot," he told her. "There was an accident near the prison."

"Oh," she said.

It was a windy October weeknight, 2007, a howling, warm night, and the chimes on the back porch banged out their high notes. "I didn't have time for lunch today," he said. He glanced down at the puddle on his plate. "This is deceptively good."

"Deceptively?"

He set down his fork. "I did everything I could to make it home in time, Tu." Tu had been shortened from Tulip long ago. She turned on the faucet. He thought to say what he should have said the moment he saw her: "I'm sorry."

Maybe she had not heard him talking with the water on.

She was wearing the black stretchy pants and the moss-green top that she always wore. Her coffee-colored hair ran in lazy waves down her back to just below her shoulder blades.

"You look pretty," he tried, probably in vain. He used to say this sort of thing to her all the time. It was the truth, no matter what old clothes she wore or her state of mind—or the filament that had gotten worn and stretched and by now just barely kept her and Lovell together. She was tall, one of the few women he had met who came within a foot of his own absurd height. She was lean but also soft, with a dancer's long neck and pale gray-green eyes and deep dimples. Still, seventeen years after she had first shown up at his apartment in Brighton with a bouquet of irises, the delivery girl for Fanciful Flowers, she was able to simply stand here and take his breath away. *I am married to an objectively beautiful woman,* he thought.

Was it shallow to reel in the presence of a woman's beauty? A little primitive?

When he had finished his dinner, Lovell brought his plate to the counter. "Go, I'll get the rest of the dishes," he said.

"Thanks." She went for the ratty yellow dish towel to dry her hands. He reached for the small of her back, but she was already off.

For years now, she had been quick to leave a room once he had entered it. Sometimes she grew jittery even when she had to stand near him; he tried but failed to remember when this had started. There may have been no sudden onset—he had to admit that there may have been the thinnest thread of chilliness when they first met years ago. He may have found it a turn-on, a challenge or something like that.

The phone rang. Hannah answered it in the next room. Lovell finished the dishes and flipped through the mail. There, beneath the water and cable bills, was their second notice from NSTAR, this time all in red type. She was the one who took care of paying the bills. Annoyed, he propped it in a little tent at the end of the counter where she would see it.

He rooted around in his briefcase for his laptop. The radiosonde data had come in yesterday from Pago Pago and his new column at *Weather* magazine was due tomorrow and he had hardly begun. A climate scientist at a foundation that studied the impact of humankind on the planet, Lovell researched the link between global warming and hurricanes. He gave himself a half hour at the computer now, no more, and then he would spend some time with the kids before they went to bed. He could work on the column tomorrow if he got to his office a little early.

As it too often did, the half hour became almost two hours, and now he and Hannah stood on either side of their bedroom, Lovell peeling off his white undershirt and she rummaging around in her dresser drawer. He watched her tug at the neck of her old sweater as if it were itchy or too tight. She finally wriggled out of it and tossed it on the floor.

They had not made love in over a year, and not for lack of trying on his part. Lovell had no idea how to turn things around at this point. They had never been the sort of couple to go at it every night, but this was an eternity, even for them.

Janine, who would be fifteen in a month, was still sawing out arpeggios on her viola next door. It had to be ten thirty or eleven.

Ethan appeared in the doorway in his robot pajamas. "I can't sleep," he said, gesturing to Janine's room. He was eight. "And the Mekenners' dog won't shut up again." This had become his nightly refrain, his attempt to stall bedtime.

"I already talked to Janine," Hannah said. "And sweetie, there's not much we can do about King." She was a good mother. She was patient when Lovell was not, anticipatory of needs and emotions that he could never predict.

Ethan replied, "You could call them."

"It's late," Hannah said. "I'm sure they're already asleep."

"So their asshole dog gets to wake up everyone else in the neighborhood?"

"Ethan," she said. "Stop listening to your sister. The mouth on her."

Behind their backs, Hannah herself could sound like a sailor.

"He does have a point," Lovell said. "King's barks can really get under your skin."

"How about one of you go ahead and pick up the phone?"

"Tu," Lovell said.

After Ethan slunk out of the room, she said, "Remember he has the orthodontist tomorrow. We find out if he'll need braces. God, I hope that doesn't bring back his stutter."

"Mm." Lovell did not remember any mention of braces.

She shot him a look—she had finely tuned radar for his not listening.

He considered reminding her of the many legitimate things that occupied him, the slew of deadlines he faced at work, the fact that this was hurricane season, that his colleague Lucinda was out all week and so he would have to cover three meetings with Ford and Chrysler over the next two days alone. But he said only, "We got another notice about the electric. We're three weeks late."

"I know," she said as she slid a sweatshirt over her head.

He waited for her to say more, and when she did not, he let other infractions pour out: the towers of recycling on the back porch, the missed tune-up for her car. "Tu, this is the third time this year that you forgot the electric. They could shut us off."

"Yeah."

"That's three notices," he repeated. She worked at most ten hours a week at the flower store. Nothing that should have bothered her did. Nothing got through to her these days.

She stretched her head from side to side, maybe working out a kink in her neck. She gazed out the window as if taking in the enormity of the starry sky.

"Is your life so busy that you can't remember to pay the bills? Can you tell me just what you do all day, every day?" He had finally said what he had only thought so many times.

She stood there in her faded Boston University sweatshirt, receiving what he had just said. "Fuck you."

"Yet something else you don't do." He moved toward the bathroom, dumbfounded. It seemed as if he had just fired a gun that he had thought was not loaded.

"Lovell," she called from the next room. "You say that to me and then you go and fucking hide? At least have the balls to look at me afterward."

Here it was, her own sailor mouth.

Something—a shoe?—hit the door behind him just as he pulled it shut. A glass bottle broke across the tile floor. He looked and saw that it had been a bottle of Coco perfume. She was wearing perfume again? Chanel had to go for a hundred bucks an ounce. She did not possess one shred of financial responsibility. She had been raised by a nanny in a waterfront estate on Martha's Vineyard. She had spent her birthdays at the Ritz in Boston or the Plaza Hotel ("You probably never read *Eloise* when you were little"). She had attended tony, off-island boarding schools. But twelve years ago, her father's business partner was convicted of embezzlement and the sailboat manufacturing company he and her father owned was liquidated. Donovan Munroe had to sell their property on the Vineyard and their brownstone in Boston, among other assets. He and Lydia moved from Edgartown into a three-bedroom Cape in Vineyard Haven. They had to stop sending Hannah money every few months, sizable checks that would arrive ostensibly for her birthday or Christmas or "a little summer fun." But she had viewed the situation with wide-eyed curiosity. Here was an opportunity for her parents—and she and Lovell, since they relied heavily on those checks at the time—to try out interesting new stores and restaurants, to warm their cold hands over a blazing fire in the living room at night, to learn to knit and sew their own clothes. Janine was a toddler at the time, and Hannah began knitting small blankets for her, thick, fuzzy hats, mittens, and socks. As their savings dwindled, Hannah agreed to apply for a part-time job at the flower store in town, where she still worked all these years later.

Lovell stared down at the shards of glass. It felt as if thousands of mites had gotten into his blood and were now nipping at him from the inside, making his heart pump at hyperspeed. It was impossible to stand still. His veins were hot.

"Every day you become more of an asshole," she called. "Lovell."

He had to steady himself.

"Lovell?"

When he returned to the room, she sat at the center of the bed, her legs crossed and her sweatshirt stretched around her knees. She looked almost nervous. "What were you doing in there? What the hell was all that?"

He would deal with the broken perfume bottle later. "Nothing," he said.

"It sounded like something."

"I just said it wasn't anything."

"You talk to me like I'm a bratty child," she said. She drew a shaky breath. "That's what you think I am—a spoiled brat."

He knew what she was doing—trying to deflect blame and distract him from the matters at hand. "Let's not have another argument about how I do or do not talk to you. Let's go over the fact that you can't even handle paying the bills. You forget to take out the *trash*. Are you depressed or something?"

"Something?" she repeated. "Do you hear how belittling you are?"

"Are you even listening to the words that I am saying? Or just the—what, the cadence of my voice?"

"The cadence says plenty."

He hauled off and kicked the bottom of the bed frame. She reached to steady herself as the bed jerked backward, waiting for him to do something worse. Janine hurried past in the hallway. He went to slam the door shut.

"Hannah," he began, tensing his leg again.

Now she looked afraid. They had gone beyond their limits. He had certainly gone beyond his. In the past, he had thrown a book or a pen at a wall and stomped around rooms, but now he was somewhere new, some menacing place with no walls or doors, no windows or light. "Listen," he said, perhaps afraid himself. "I want to understand. I really do. Why is everything so hard for you? I mean in terms of work and daily life and even us. I genuinely want to know." It was not ideal to conflate all their problems this way—money, sex, moods, life—but he could not help it. They had become indivisible.

Her fear looked to be dissipating. "Obviously," she said, "you think I should work more hours. Forget about the fact that I can't stand that goddamned store anymore. I've worked at some florist for the majority of my adult life, and at this point I can't think of one good reason why."

She had said this sort of thing countless times before. She seemed to blame him for her own failure to choose a more meaningful career.

"What job would you rather have?"

"If I knew, don't you think I'd be doing it? I'm almost forty. I can't exactly dream up some new life and, poof, just start over." She swept her hand across her forehead as if she were onstage. "Oh, my whole life feels like an epilogue right now."

This was rich. "Who really says that? Some woman in a cheesy movie? A character in a goddamned novel?"

Hannah made a gusting sound, as if she had been punched in the stomach.

"You have to decide to make it better. Right, Tu? No?" She had never had to work for anything. She had never been tasked with propelling her own life anywhere. She complained incessantly about what little work she actually did. Maybe he had reason to sound indifferent. "You just make a decision and go with it."

"How do I do that?"

What was he supposed to say now? *My whole life feels like an epilogue.* Didn't her life include him? He just shook his head.

"Thank you, as always, Lovell, for your stunning compassion and understanding."

He was not about to let her continue playing the martyr. "Chanel? Really?"

"Keep it down. You want the kids to hear you?" she said. She had a point. The kids had heard plenty tonight—and over the years. "Wait, is that what you dropped? Or did you do something to it? You did something."

"We are not people who can afford Chanel."

"Oh God. It was my only perfume. Sophie bought it for me the last time they went to Paris to visit her parents." Sophie Vallard, her college roommate, had grown up in France. "Why am I justifying anything to *you*?"

"And you call me belittling?" he said, burning inside. "You're the one who secretly looks down on me. You're the one who's the almighty princess here."

"Yeah? And you are a big fucking loser." She rose and took a step toward the bathroom. "No, you know what? You broke it, you clean it up." She reached for a pillow and held it to her chest. She kept her eyes on the mattress. She appeared to be deciding on the best way to continue—or whether to continue at all. She stood and walked out of the room.

Every molecule of rage flew away from him. He wanted to take back all that he had said.

He went to the window to see whether she was now in her car, peeling out of the driveway, but both of their cars sat side by side in the darkened driveway, unoccupied. He waited a moment to see whether she would appear below, but she did not, and so he went to lie down.

He faced Hannah's pillow, bunched into a ball in its ivory case at the far corner of the mattress. The poison that they kept stored away inside themselves, this toxic stew that had expanded for years, had finally boiled over and out.

He had suggested marriage counseling maybe six months ago. "Couples' therapy?" Hannah had asked with a sour look. She had been to therapists before, someone while at Boston University, then another therapist in Cambridge soon after she and Lovell had met—and he had thought the timing of those particular sessions strange. "Don't take it personally. And anyway, he asks me all the same questions I ask myself. When I say that I don't know, he just asks me why not, and it goes on and on like that, pretty much nowhere." "But that was years ago," he had said. She did not seem to know who she was anymore or, perhaps worse, who she wanted to be. "You need to figure out what you want out of life," he had said. She had replied, "So you're saying that I'm the only one who needs help?"

Janine pushed the door open an inch and leaned her face forward. She peered around the room. Her hair sat in a brutalized tangle at the top of her head. "You all done?" she asked.

"Yes," he said, unable to face her right now. "Let's get you back to sleep," he managed. If he was able to seem calm and steady, she might believe that he was.

"I wasn't sleeping," she said, keeping herself behind the door as he approached.

"Of course not. I'm sorry. That was no good." He had learned that the more he tried to explain away their battles to her, the worse they sounded.

"Where's Mom?"

Hannah slept in Ethan's room whenever he had trouble sleeping, which was most nights. "Probably in your brother's room."

Janine stepped carefully around the door and in front of him. "Is she OK?" His daughter could be surprisingly maternal toward Hannah.

"Your mother's fine," he said automatically. "I'm fine too," he added, not that she had asked.

He followed her to her bedroom. He tucked her in, although she flinched at his touch, and then he sat beside her on her mattress. At last she closed her eyes.

He stayed a moment, looking down at his daughter, the wisps of light hair across her temple, her lips barely parted as she lay there on her side. She may not have been sleeping, she may have been pretending, but he did not say anything. He was grateful that she allowed this right now, that she was letting him just stay here and look at her.

THE EARLY DAYS. Those first few months of friendship when all that he knew of Hannah Munroe fit inside a daydream. She had grown up on Martha's Vineyard and now lived alone in one of her parents' two off-island homes, a four-bedroom brownstone on Clarendon, where a tree-size grandfather clock stood guard just inside the front door. She kept a rosewood box of Burdick's honey caramel truffles on her coffee table at all times. She collected antique glass perfume bottles that were rounded and spiny, swirled with primordial indigo

and deep, opaque emerald. She was passionate about the Red
Sox but hated the Patriots and football in general. She gave the
impression of a swan: regal but fragile, lovely and thoughtful
and capable of sudden wildness. She was the most feminine,
self-assured, compelling female that he had ever met.

She called him one night with a ticket to a game against the
Blue Jays the next afternoon. "My friend just backed out. I'd
have called you sooner," she began.

He immediately accepted, and because she had a car and he
did not, they agreed that she would come pick him up before
the game.

The next afternoon, she arrived at his apartment in Brighton
wearing a ski jacket, her neck swaddled in a lumpy, hairy scarf.
Her nostrils were pink and inflamed and she sounded congested. Had he missed it over the phone? He led her inside
and offered to make her some tea. "We don't have to leave
this second, do we?"

"No." She shrugged. "Not just yet."

He hung up her jacket while she unraveled her scarf. He
filled a mug with water and put it in the microwave. They sat
across from each other at the wobbly card table in his kitchen.
Down the hall, his roommate, Paul, labored with his trombone
scales, unable to reach the higher notes.

Hannah's hair pooled onto her shoulders and ran over her
small breasts, down over her stomach, stopping at her waist.
She had these light-filled eyes, and a black eyelash clung to the

side ridge of her nose. She made considerable attempts to sniff back all that was inside her sinuses.

He went to find a box of tissues, and when he returned he asked, "You sure you're up for a baseball game outside?"

"I'll be fine. The season's almost over—we have to go. Thanks," she said as she reached for the box. In vain she tried again to release the blockage. She wadded up the dry tissue and stuffed it in her pants pocket. She asked, "Have you ever been in love?"

Her crazy questions—always non sequiturs—still blind-sided him. "I'm not sure. I don't think so."

Paul groaned and started again at the beginning of his scale. The microwave beeped and Lovell found a box of Lipton that Paul's mother had left on her last visit. Lovell set the mug down before Hannah and she brought it to her mouth for a dainty sip. The table tottered beneath her arm and she wrapped her fingers around the mug to protect the tea or her lap. He found an empty box of Frosted Flakes with the recycling, folded it into awkward fourths, and jammed it under the shortest table leg. Once he took his seat again, she looked off beyond him.

"So, what exactly does it feel like?" he said at last.

"Oh, you'd know."

"That's what they always say—'you just know.'"

The trombone grew louder, a whiny, embarrassing little brother in the next room—*I'm here, I'm here, I'm here.*

"The first night I met him, we slept together," she said. This jerk named Doug Bowen had been her fiancé just a few months ago. She talked about him a lot. "And the next night too. I probably shouldn't admit that."

How to respond? Anyway, Lovell had a chemical oceanography paper due the next day. He should have been finalizing his isotope indicators. Proofreading. He had a hundred things he should have been doing other than sitting here with this girl.

"You've never done that? Slept with someone right away?" She made one last heartbreaking attempt to breathe through her nose.

He had, but he didn't think it was love, nothing like that. "What's the right answer?"

"There's no right or wrong."

"I guess there was this one girl and we almost did. We got really close," he said. "But I didn't want to hurt her later on, so I held off. I mean we both did."

"Ah, the right answer anyway."

He watched her guide the tea bag around the water by its paper tag. He was a gawky, long-limbed PhD candidate from semirural Maine. He was allergic to shellfish, and in his rare free time he did little other than monopolize his roommate's Nintendo. She was light years out of his league.

"Now the wrong answer," she said.

"Yes, we went ahead and slept together, but I didn't really love her."

"Tell me more."

"She—" he began. A section of his chest withered. He felt protective of it. "Naw."

"No?"

He shook his head.

"Good for you." She nodded. "Really. It's none of my business." She finished her tea and drew a deep breath, this time through her mouth. She sat up straighter and looked at him anew, as if only now realizing that he was in the room with her, Lovell and not someone else. "You're a good person, aren't you?"

"I try," he said.

She studied his face, side to side, up and down. "I could use a good person. I need someone good in my life right now."

"*Good,*" he said sadly. He had landed on that brotherly side of the spectrum.

"Oh."

"'Oh' what?" His face was hot. It was too late.

"Nothing," she said carefully. But she half smiled— embarrassed? Maybe, hopefully, intrigued? "Are we ready to go?"

LOVELL CHECKED ONE more time to see whether both cars were in the driveway. When he saw that they were, he headed downstairs for his laptop and answered some work e-mails. There would be no point trying to fall asleep after this night. He skimmed the newspaper, considered finding his banjo, which he had not played in a few years. He flipped through some magazines.

He eventually made his way back upstairs and into bed. Later he heard the Mekenner kid on his bike outside and the smack of newspapers landing on driveways, as well as the sound of the milk truck screeching down Winter Street, that compact, joyless, bovine woman (Hannah's term—it made him howl) who left bottles of organic milk on people's porches once a week.

In the morning, Hannah remained steely for the brief time that he saw her before he had to leave for work. But she allowed him to give her a quick kiss good-bye, and he hoped this might be a precursor to a truce.

He turned his thoughts to all that lay ahead of him at his office: the numbers from Pago Pago would screw up his estimates of potential intensity and of tropical cyclones, as well as his data proving that increases in sea surface temperatures had to be associated with spikes in potential intensity. Hurricane Katrina had garnered him and his theory some attention, but there were still plenty of naysayers in the government. Lovell arrived at Mass Environmental and the day began.

Chapter 2

Thirty hours after he had kissed Hannah good-bye and headed off for work, Lovell waited, his chest pounding, on the front steps of a brick bunker, where by a set of automatic glass doors he met Bob Duncan, a short, doughy detective with sprawling black eyebrows and a crushing handshake.

"You're not a small man," Duncan said, looking up at Lovell's face.

"My parents are both tall." At six feet five inches, he heard this sort of thing all the time, but it sounded kind of different now.

He followed the detective into an overheated office barely large enough for its desk and two metal chairs. Lovell had contacted the police himself this morning and reported her missing. He had had no idea what else to do. Should he have come out and told the kids that she was quite likely in the process of leaving him? She had taken off once about a year ago and spent the night at her sister's, although she did return early the next morning, before the kids woke.

Duncan had already spoken with Janine and several of Lovell's coworkers and Ethan and one of his teachers, who had seen Hannah yesterday morning. Lovell knew that the detective had talked to Sophie, whom Hannah had called that morning, and even a neighbor, who had confirmed that Lovell's car had remained in the driveway during the nights before and after she went missing. Wasn't interrogating the neighbors and the rest of them a little much? A thought materialized: What if one of them had heard his and Hannah's exchange? What if the kids had said something to Duncan?

The detective had called about an hour ago and had asked Lovell to come down to the station and bring one of Hannah's hairbrushes, "one full of hair, if you've got it." Duncan said that a bracelet, maybe hers, had turned up. A hairbrush? A bracelet? Lovell had thought that this was beginning to sound more like an investigation than a search effort.

Now Duncan said, "Just so you know, we found the bracelet on a beach in South Boston."

"Southie?"

"Yep," he said. "Carson Beach. Be right back . . ." He left Lovell alone.

Lovell dropped his eyes to the eggplant-colored carpet. The room was still. He had the sensation of standing alone in the eye of a storm. Every second of this grew stranger and more unnerving. He thought for some reason of Boston University and Doug Bowen. Neither had anything to do with South Boston, as far as he knew.

Lovell had given Hannah several bracelets over the years. Had she gone for a walk and, thinking back on that last night, decided to heave one of them into the ocean?

Duncan returned and handed Lovell a heavy plastic bag with a bracelet inside. The silver links, the small amber beads. He had gotten her this one for their last wedding anniversary. Lovell's mouth went dry. The detective waited, his thumbs dug into his pants pockets.

Lovell set the bag on the desk. "Yes," he finally said.

"Any reason she might have been in Southie?"

"I was just trying to figure that out. We don't know anyone there."

Duncan made his mouth impossibly small and clapped his hands together. "One of the girls at the flower store? Hannah called her to say she was running late for work because Janine was home sick."

"Janine wasn't home sick," Lovell said.

"We know. Hannah made the call from Boston," the detective said. "You look a little sick yourself, Mr. Hall."

Lovell blinked. "Please call me Lovell. I have no idea where my wife is right now. I'm standing here in a police station identifying her bracelet. So yes, I don't feel so well. Do you have people searching South Boston?"

"Can you give me your best guess why Hannah might have driven herself to Carson Beach?"

"I honestly—I'm telling the truth—I have no idea," Lovell said. The argument might explain some part of what was going on right now but certainly not everything. "I assume you checked with her sister? Her parents?"

"We did."

"I know you talked to her friend Sophie. None of them knew anything?"

"Not a thing." Duncan cleared his throat. "Jeez, you really are tall. I guess Hannah's tall too for a woman, but not as big as you are."

Lovell almost wished this man would come out and accuse him of something.

If he admitted that they'd had an explosive exchange the night before she left, if Lovell admitted that Hannah may well be off somewhere planning her next move, deciding whether to even stay married to him, the police would probably halt their search. If they had even begun it. He would rather have them drag her back home to him than leave her alone out there, pissed off or defeated or distressed and vulnerable in some place that might not be all that safe.

"Any other insights you can give us?" Duncan asked.

"I guess not," Lovell finally said.

"Need you to sign this," the detective said, beginning to shuffle through a stack of papers on his desk. He handed

Lovell a ballpoint pen and a clipboard that held a triplicate form onto which his alibi had been typed. He had been at work during the time Hannah disappeared, save the twenty minutes he went out to grab lunch and the brief time later when he had to get something he had left in his car. Lovell signed his name. Duncan muttered his thanks and told him they would be in touch.

THAT EVENING, ETHAN came and crawled onto his father's lap on the couch, though he hardly fit anymore. "Come sit with us?" Lovell asked Janine, patting the space next to them.

She sat across from them in an easy chair with her chin resting on her knees. She shook her head, her eyes on the floor. She had been uncharacteristically subdued since yesterday. Her tangled sand-colored hair fell around her face and down her shoulders. With her wide jaw and thin, jutting nose, she resembled Lovell more than Hannah. Ethan had inherited his mother's looks.

"I'm scared," Ethan finally said.

Lovell wrapped his arms around his son, his heart thumping against Ethan's narrow back. "I know." He could not think of how to set their minds at ease.

Yesterday afternoon, Ethan's teacher phoned him at the office to ask why no one had come for pickup. "He's been waiting here for an hour," she told him. Lovell hurried to close out of a labyrinthine power dissipation model at work and, perplexed and miffed, drove during the onset of rush hour to pick up Ethan.

Lovell threw together a dinner of grilled cheese and deflected the kids' questions about Hannah in whatever way he could, trying to hide the wave of dread mounting within him. He surreptitiously peered around the kitchen and living room for some note or clue, a missing suitcase or toiletries. Her car was gone, her jacket and purse too, but nothing else, as far as he could tell. He assured the kids that she would show up soon or at least call, of course she would. She had probably forgotten about some old friend's birthday, he told them, or a dinner with her sister. The two met for dinner or drinks every month or so. The kids appeared to buy it, as did Lovell to some extent after a while. "If you can, try not to worry," he told them.

After three games of Boggle and a repeat episode of *Nova* about the spread of eelgrass in some coastal California lagoon, after more secret searches of every room in the house, including their basement, he ushered the kids upstairs to bed and promised to send Hannah directly to their rooms the minute she got home so that she could kiss them good night.

He kept his arms tight around Ethan's now.

A commercial for Mr. Clean was on the TV. Janine picked at a Band-Aid around her finger. "How come it's always women in these ads for cleaning shit?"

"Language," Lovell said.

"No men clean their houses?"

"That's a woman's job," Lovell tried to joke. She saw everything in black and white, and sometimes it was difficult not to parody.

"You're hilarious," she deadpanned. It was unfortunately true: he rarely picked up a mop or a broom.

"That policeman asked me what we talked about in the car when she drove me to school that morning," Ethan said. He wriggled free from Lovell's arms. "And where I thought she might be, like a million questions about all the places she goes and people she sees and why—like he thought I was keeping something secret." He went back to the beanbag that he had brought downstairs from his bedroom.

"They did?" Lovell said. "Did they ask you anything about our family or, or about me?"

"Just whether you guys ever fought or anything."

"What did you say?"

"I don't know."

Janine watched Lovell.

"I said I guess so, that sometimes you guys argued."

Lovell exhaled. He supposed Ethan could have said worse. Ethan or Janine may well have heard only pieces of what was said, pieces that without context would have sounded awful. Lovell was too often mistaken by members of his family for what he was not: self-absorbed rather than thoughtful; blunt, not honest; impatient, not logical. It was idiocy. What had Janine told the policeman? Lovell was afraid to ask her.

They watched TV quietly for a while, but he could hardly

sit still. He hated that he was forced to view his own kids with suspicion right now. He hated that he was secretly agonizing about himself.

If nothing else, he reminded himself, he had his alibi. *Southie. Carson Beach.* It was not a place where Hannah would have gone. She would have driven to Gloucester or Rockport, where she and Sophie used to go in college, if she wanted a walk on the beach. He finally rose and went to the kitchen. Had she ever gone to Carson while at BU? He estimated the distance from her parents' old town house to the beach.

He scrubbed spots of Janine's yogurt off the kitchen counter and then swept the tile floor. He made his way to the front hall and paced back and forth, his head down, his eyes on his feet.

When he looked up, a beam of light poured through the window by the door. A woman with a microphone was standing on the sidewalk, a cameraman next to her. Was that Susan Sperck from the local news? Strange. He remembered that a house a few blocks away had burned down just the other week. Maybe there was another fire in the neighborhood. He switched on the porch light and moved closer to the window.

She met his eyes and moved down his front walk toward him. "What is this?" he said.

She was shorter in person than he might have thought. Stout and pink-faced, her fine tan hair cut in a severe bob, she lifted the microphone up and beside her head. The man who carried the cumbersome black camera scrambled to catch up with her.

Lovell stepped outside.

"Lovell Hall?" she said into her microphone. She introduced herself briefly. "What do you think happened to your wife?" She held the top of the microphone toward him. The man behind her hefted the camera onto his shoulder and began to film.

Had Bob Duncan or someone else at the police station told her about Hannah? "Hold on," Lovell finally said. He closed the door behind him before the kids could see or hear any more and turned back to her. "I wish I knew."

"What have the police told you?"

"I don't think—I mean, I probably shouldn't—" he said. "What do *you* know?"

The cameraman shifted on his feet.

"Where were you when she went missing?" Susan Sperck continued.

"What?" he managed.

"Can you tell me where you were that day?"

"I don't believe I am required to tell you that," he said. He added, "But I was at work. At my office in Cambridge. You can call the police if you'd like to confirm it."

"We'll do that. Do the police have any leads?"

"I don't know—I mean, not that I know of."

"Well, what do you know?"

The kids would be wondering where he was. For all he knew, they were standing in the front hallway, watching this through the window beside the door. "I have to get back to my family," he finally said. "The police can answer any other questions. Good night."

He moved back inside and closed the door behind him, thoroughly rattled, trying to understand exactly what had just happened and what this entailed. If only he could know that Hannah was at least, if nothing else, safe.

Janine appeared at the other end of the hallway, peering past him to see what was outside.

"It was someone from Channel Six," he said slowly.

"What did they want?"

"Oh, just, well, they somehow heard about Mom and just wanted to make sure we were doing OK," he said. "No big deal."

"Were you actually on TV?"

"They did ask me a couple questions."

"How did they know about this? Did something happen to Mom? What the fuck, Dad?"

He took a few steps toward her. "News reporters try to turn everything into a story. Their showing up here doesn't mean a thing. Listen, Mom will be fine. She'll come back soon."

"I really hope so," she said. She drew a lock of her hair through and out the side of her mouth. "You didn't tell me if you were on TV."

"They interviewed me, but who knows if they'll actually air it. I didn't really have much to say. I'm sure they'll see that there's no real news story here and dump the two minutes of footage they got of me."

She appeared to consider and accept what he had said. "So what do we do now?"

He thought a moment. "Get ready for bed?"

"It's only eight thirty."

"What about your homework?" Most evenings he spent at the kitchen table behind his computer or talking on the phone to researchers in Perth or Hong Kong, where the time difference made it impossible to speak during his workday. Apparently he had only had a vague sense of his children's typical nights.

"Tomorrow is Saturday," she said.

"All right," he said, gesturing for Ethan, nearby on his beanbag, to join him. "Let's see if there's a movie on TV." He flicked around, trying to find something that would appeal to their different ages and tastes, something calming or funny, but since it was October, all he could find were horror movies. "Perfect," Lovell said as, on the screen, Anthony Hopkins sucked the air through his teeth. Lovell poked the "off" button on the remote again and again, but the batteries must have died. "Jesus Christ."

"Language," said Ethan.

Lovell finally stood and pressed the power button below the screen. "Who wants to play Uno?" he asked weakly.

IN THE MORNING, Susan Sperck had gone, but a couple of news vans were now parked along the street across from his house. Thankfully, it was a Saturday, and Janine and Ethan could stay home. They had all shared his bed last night and none of them had gotten much rest, so Lovell let the kids sleep in and went downstairs to call Duncan. "Any updates on the case?"

"Nothing to tell."

"A reporter came by last night," Lovell said. "And now some more are parked on our street."

"I haven't talked to any of them. But I guess I'm not all that surprised. Some bored cop with a big mouth. You know. And the prettier the lady, the wider the coverage."

Lovell winced.

"I'll talk to the guys."

"I'd appreciate it." He glanced out his living room window as two more news vans pulled up behind the others. "And if you wouldn't mind giving me a heads-up next time you talk to my kids, I'd appreciate that as well. They're pretty freaked out right now." Lovell added, "We all are."

"I'll do what I can," Duncan said. "Oh, and Lovell, if I were you, I wouldn't talk to any more reporters. Just ignore them, if you can. Pretend they're not there."

Are you kidding? Lovell nearly said. How easy it must be to dole out glib advice at times like these.

The phone rang throughout the day: Hannah's parents and sister, each with rapid-fire questions about when he had last seen her and orders to check this place and that ("Of course I checked the shop") and suggestions for others that he might not have considered; her closest friends; a few of his coworkers who had seen the news. His mother called and asked him whether he might be forgetting some place where Hannah liked to go. "Why does everyone say that? It's not as if you're going to suddenly jog my memory by making me feel like an idiot."

"*Lovell.*"

Janine sat across the room, eyeing him.

"I'm sorry," he said. "This isn't easy."

"How are the kids doing?" his mother tried. "Are people really asking you why you don't know more?"

"Mom." No one in his immediate family—his mother, father, or brother—was particularly sensitive. They were all academics, such logical people, tortoises whose shells shut away their hearts—feeble from such infrequent use—deep within them and allowed only their heads, their brains, out in the wide, strange world to make sense of it all. Anyway, his mother knew nothing of the state of his marriage other than the little friction that she had witnessed herself, from what he could remember—just a few hushed arguments that she would never have registered.

"I'm headed out to Costco," she said after a moment. "You want me to bring you toilet paper or anything?"

"I have no idea," he said automatically. "I'm not the one who inventories that stuff."

"I'll just get you some. You can never have too much."

Everyone who had heard that Hannah disappeared called that day, it seemed, but Detective Duncan. There had to have been ten vans outside his house by the time the sun began to set, maybe more.

Lovell went for a bottle of Grey Goose. He stood in the front hallway, watching a circle of people chat beside his mailbox. Susan Sperck appeared at the side of the group, a cell phone to her ear. Someone next to her nodded toward the front door, and Lovell moved back before any of the reporters could see him.

Chapter 3

Hannah woke alone in her son's bed. Lovell had made coffee. She could almost taste it—hazelnut, her favorite—as she pulled Ethan's comforter around her shoulders, but as she rose further toward consciousness, she remembered all that had happened last night. Was making coffee enough of an apology? After all that he had done and almost done—his aimless rage, the embarrassing violence like a rotten smell throughout the room—and all that he had said, which was worse than his physical bluster, all that he had verbalized to try to make her smaller, just this piddling thing, hardly worth a listen, her empty days, her lazy disregard for bills and cars and recycling. He was stunted, too male, too myopic to comprehend that the piddling things were in fact those bills and cars and recycling, not her. Or had she given so much of her life to those eviscerating tasks and gotten to be, herself, just as eviscerating? The line of thinking was old and tired. There was nothing new about women despising their drudgery. There was nothing new about women wanting more. On and on she went like this. Coffee. It was a kid dropping his eyes and mouthing, "Sorry," to the ground. Lovell was impossible. Being married to him had become impossible, and this sensation bled into the rest of her life and made her feel as if she had become someone else, someone she hardly knew and did not like.

She heard Ethan in the hallway and Janine in the shower and Beethoven on that iPod and speaker she carried from room to room. Hannah worried for her daughter, the world the way it was, boys, girls, friends, love, sex, heartbreak, all of it. Hannah wondered whether her daughter had enough people in her life—enough friends. She gravitated toward young children—she was a sought-after babysitter in the neighborhood—or adults instead of kids her own age. She was her father's daughter; friendships with her peers came a distant third, in Janine's case, after homework and viola. Being likable was not a priority for her.

It was Thursday. Hannah had to work at the flower shop later that morning, and Ethan's orthodontist appointment was in the afternoon. She stretched and unwound the sheet from her body.

Janine stood alone in the kitchen at the counter, her back hunched. It drove Hannah crazy, the girl's consistently bad posture. Janine wore her black army pants and a green button-down cardigan draped over an old white T-shirt. Clothes did not interest her. Maybe it was in fact her height: not much fit her.

At Janine's age, Hannah had already been tall too, taller than the other girls in her class. Her mother had always said, "You could easily do commercials—print *or* TV. Soon you'll be able to do runway. Say the word and I'll call some old contacts," and Hannah's friends always told her, "I wish I was that tall. Do you know how lucky you are?" Janine called commercials the "tools of a sexist corporate culture," thanks to a new media literacy class at her school. Hannah's response was, "Well, yes. Doesn't everyone already know that?"

Janine slouched at the table and glanced over at her. "You OK, Mom?"

"I'm fine." Hannah shuddered to think of her listening to Lovell crash around last night like a big, dumb bear caught inside the house. "You look nice today," Hannah tried. Everyone wanted to hear that, didn't they?

Janine shrugged and reached for a mug of coffee on the table.

"You shouldn't drink coffee," Hannah said. "You're too young."

"It'll stunt my growth, right? I'd be fine with that."

"Tall can be pretty. You are pretty, you know," Hannah tried. She looked around the pantry for a box of bran flakes and brought the cereal and a bowl to the table. Janine pulled a strand of long, limp hair toward her mouth. She had this new habit of chewing the hair that hung beside her face, and the ends had gotten matted and wet. Hannah said, "Sweetie, don't suck on your hair."

Janine reached for her coffee. Her body was lanky but at the same time chubby, stretched here and compressed there. She had not taken well to adolescence. Then again, who did? Well, Hannah herself, of course. But maybe to be happy at fourteen was to be happy too soon, to use up something that was, in the end, finite.

At least Ethan had a few more years before the hormones flooded in. Of course these years would pass in a moment. His ninth birthday was approaching, and she wanted to do something that he would always remember before he too turned sullen and sulky—decorate the house like a spaceship, ask all his friends to dress as aliens or something. Lovell had laughed at the idea. "Seems a little much."

Hannah stepped behind Janine and kissed the top of her damp head. "Being tall is a good thing. Someday you'll see." She continued, "Coffee isn't good for you."

"You drink it," Janine said. She opened the social studies textbook beside her place mat.

Lovell blazed into the kitchen and accidentally knocked a banana off the counter. He leaned down to peck Hannah goodbye. He said he was late for a meeting. The kitchen was never clean; he always dropped things and left messes throughout the house. She watched him searching for his keys, but looked away before he could see her. What if he had gone ahead and hit her last night? But then he would have become someone else, someone at least formidable, a significant threat. A legitimate problem. She no longer loved him. She may never have loved him.

She poured cereal into a bowl and asked Janine, "Are you going to the library later to work on that civil rights paper?"

Janine turned a page.

"Hello?"

"I'll go after school."

"What time should I pick you up?"

Janine stared at the words before her.

"What time?"

"Shit. I don't know, four?"

"Language. Four o'clock on the front steps. Don't be late— Ethan has the orthodontist at four thirty." Hannah dug her spoon into the bowl and tried to finish the cereal before the flakes wilted in the milk.

Janine left her mug on the table and slid her books into her backpack. She twisted her hair into a frayed ponytail. "Bye," she said, and she ran outside to her bus stop. Hannah looked over at the mug she had left, the brown droplets halfway down the side.

Ethan remained upstairs in his room. "Eth. You ready?" she called up to him. "We need to go." She waited for an answer. "Eth, come on, let's get going," she said, but so what if he missed a day of school? So what if he lounged around the house? What if they all abandoned their duties and did what they wanted today—watched TV, ate sugary cereal, read comic books? Ethan would ride his unicycle around the driveway. Janine would practice viola. Lovell would set up his computer and maps all over the kitchen table. Or he would putter around the house or up on the roof, tending to the solar panels. And Hannah? If she could do anything she wanted today, anything at all? She didn't know. She had no idea.

On the counter was a folder of old photos her mother had given her yesterday, pictures of Hannah as a child that had not made it into an album. She opened the folder and flipped through them. There was her first-grade picture, another of her steering her father's boat. She stopped at a shot of her sitting in her father's office chair behind his big mahogany desk, her hair in yellow plastic barrettes with little chicks. She didn't remember this one. She did remember the few times that she went to that office overlooking the ferry dock, Mrs. Corcoran, the pudgy, kindly secretary who let Hannah try on her red bifocals, the other men flashing by, oblivious, leaving only the whiff of cigarettes. And the objects of the place: her father's glass paperweight with the tiny sailboat inside; his envelope opener, that bronze dagger; the supply closet, the wondrous supply closet that held boxes of shiny clips and erasers and highlighters that Mrs. Corcoran allowed her to play with in the waiting area. A five- or six-year-old Hannah smiled back at her with all the hope and imagination in the world. It took her breath away. Hannah slipped the folder into her purse. She did not want to see that picture for a while.

Ethan was before her, his jacket zipped to his chin, his back-pack hanging from his shoulders.

"Good job," she said. "You're all set."

He nodded and she gathered him in her arms. He smelled of grape toothpaste and bubble-gum shampoo, and blessedly he let her hold him for a long moment. She grabbed a granola bar for him and ushered him out the front door.

Chapter 4

On Sunday morning, while the kids were still asleep, Lovell went to make coffee. He took note of the sprinkle of grounds that had remained beside the coffee maker since Hannah's disappearance four mornings ago. She preferred flavored; he, "regular leaded," as he called it. Making her favorite coffee that morning must have done nothing for her, in the end.

He still half expected, half hoped, that he would hear the sound of the front door opening and Hannah calling, *Hello? Anyone home?* Her arms full of gifts or flowers to convey a change of heart, maybe contrition, she would say that she had just needed some time and space apart from him in order to really think things over and come to the decision that she did not—of course she did not—want to leave them.

He turned on the coffee maker and waited, hands laced

around the back of his neck, for the sound of the gurgling water to fill the silence in the kitchen. Once it did, he walked outside to get the newspaper, shielding his face from the reporters, but when he looked, he saw that the TV crews had packed up their equipment and gone home. He reminded himself that there had been no news about the case for two days now. Curled leaves blew in little horizontal tornadoes down the street. The sidewalks were empty.

He moved toward the front lawn to pick up some fallen branches from a recent storm and saw a young couple pass by on the sidewalk. They averted their eyes at first, but the woman peered back over at him. He had no idea how to behave, how to look, or what, if anything, to say when people watched him this way. Yesterday, Karen Mekenner had inched past his house in her silver Volvo, eyeing him as he took out the trash.

Moving here from their overpriced, cramped Brookline studio had been a reasonable idea so many years ago. The price was low, the town quaint and pretty. In the summers, they could bike to Walden Pond or go apple picking in Stow.

They, or Hannah really, "could not have anticipated the obliterating quiet, the aloofness but at the same time awkwardness of so many of the people here, the deep homogeneity and stunning averageness," as she once put it in an e-mail to him on a particularly low day. Lovell had not been around enough over the years for these things to really bother him. "The ruddy-faced men in finance, the athletic stay-at-home moms, the fucking Boy Scouts, the golden retrievers, the gas-guzzling minivans, the holiday-themed flags near the front door for any and every holiday." She had gone on writing in this manner, as if for some phantom reader who did not in fact live in the same town. "Time must have stopped moving forward here in this suburb. It seems like the civil rights movement and sexual revolution never reached this place."

Most of the women she had met here were nice enough. They seemed to want to be her friend—they eagerly approached her at school events and music classes, they invited her to moms' nights out and various in-home parties where kitchenware or makeup was being sold, but in the end they seemed to Hannah more like coworkers than friends. She certainly never lit up when with them the way she did with Sophie or the others. She'd had a small gaggle of close friends from her high school and BU, these affable, generous, funny women. Most of them lived elsewhere now; only Sophie was still in Massachusetts. A few times Hannah had suggested trips to visit the others in San Francisco or even London, but Lovell reminded her that they could never afford the flights, not if they expected to pay their mortgage and save for the kids to go to college.

He turned back to his house, the stained, angled modern that held three solar panels across its slanted roof. Yellow plastic rain barrels sat under drain spouts and dribbled water onto the mulch beneath. In this neighborhood of pristine Cape Cods and Victorians, each set squarely on an identical plot of plush green grass, their house sometimes looked to him as if it had been dropped here by mistake.

LATER THAT EVENING, the three of them and his mother, who had come with dinner, sat over a game of Scrabble. Joanne Hall, a lanky woman with a cap of coarse gray hair, set down tiles that spelled QUANTUM. So far, she had spelled SUBSET, ZETA, and ZERO. She was a theoretical mathematician at MIT.

"You're kicking ass, Grandma," Janine said.

Joanne shrugged with false modesty.

"Mom," Lovell whispered to her. "Can't you let one of them win right now?"

"Why?"

"Do I have to explain it?"

She reached for the box of Entenmann's brownies that she had brought for dessert and set it beside them. "I told your father I'd check in with him around now," she said to Lovell, and she went off to the living room to make the call.

"Do you miss Mom?" Ethan asked him, as if they had just been discussing Hannah. "Are you worried about her?"

"Yes. Eth, of course I do," Lovell said.

"You don't talk about it," Janine said.

"Do I have to?"

"No, you don't *have* to, Dad," she said.

"*You* guys miss her right now," Lovell said.

Ethan nodded. Janine watched her father.

Lovell added, "She never liked Scrabble. She was more of a card game person."

"We know," Janine said.

"She slept in my bed with me on her last night," Ethan said.

Lovell had not really broached with them the daunting subject of that night. He held his hands tight together in his lap and began: "I wish that night had been different. You guys have to know this. You can love someone and be angry at them. Grown-ups fight sometimes. Married people argue. They just do." There was conviction in his voice. He had to at least try to maintain this stance, both for them and for himself: *No marriage is easy.* All couples go through difficult times. "She'll come back soon. Someone will find her. She'll be totally and completely fine."

Janine did not take her eyes off him. She studied him as he reached for the felt bag of letters, as he pulled out three and set them in the little plastic holder and said, "Janine, your turn."

She picked up a brownie. "I'm going to sit out this round," she said at last.

Chapter 5

Hannah was late bringing Ethan to school. Sarah, one of the teaching assistants, waited alone for him by the red double doors. She ushered Ethan inside and glanced back to wave at Hannah, who was standing against her car at the curb. Sarah had blond hair cut in a matronly style and wore a blondish sweater and loose tan pants. She was pretty and pleasant. Hannah waved back at Sarah and thought to ask her whether she needed any help today, but in less than a moment the two had disappeared inside.

The sun shone fiercely and the sky was cloudless, the sidewalk black, newly paved. Not one other person could be seen. Children everywhere were in school. Hannah looked at her watch—she had two and a half hours before she was due at work. She rushed up the concrete stairs and inside the school to catch up with Sarah and Ethan.

"Forget something?" Sarah asked.

"I've got some time before I have to be at work. Do you guys need any help this morning with snack or recess?" Ethan looked at his feet.

"Thanks, but I think we're all set." Sarah enunciated and spoke a half beat too slowly, in the way that women who worked with small children did. "We have a full day planned. We're making volcanoes. Papier-mâché."

"Oh. Good, that sounds fun."

Sarah smiled. "Messy fun."

Hannah's face prickled with heat. "Then I'll go enjoy this time to myself and leave you guys to it." She started back down the hallway.

The other week, after volunteering in Ethan's class, she had seen a kindergartner seated against the wall outside a classroom, his arms around his knees. The boy had an older brother in Ethan's grade, and Hannah had heard that the father had just left their family. "You all right?" Hannah had asked, and he shrugged, his tangled black hair nearly covering his face.

Hannah glanced around. "You want some company? Are you in time-out or something?"

He was silent, but he revealed enough of his face for Hannah to see that he was crying.

"I could sit with—"

"Go away."

"Okay," Hannah said. She buttoned up her coat and hurried off, and when she had reached the front doors of the school, she called Lovell at work and told him about the boy.

"Just let it be," he said.

"I guess. You don't think I should tell the teacher what's going on in their house? She might not know yet. You should have seen this kid. He looked awful. He's so little."

"I don't know. I guess you could tell her."

She heard him begin to type, and said, "Forget it."

"He'll be fine," Lovell said vacantly.

"I was thinking about Tunis the other day," she said. Just the mention of the place where they had gone for their honeymoon always drew him back.

"Yeah?"

"Do you remember that woman singing? And her husband, that doctor, called her a cow or something like that? And that creepy basement! God, that was scary."

"Given our situation, I wasn't paying much attention."

"And then sleeping in that Bedouin tent in the desert."

"Ah. That was much better."

"Our nomad? What was his name?"

"Dhia? Daly? I don't remember."

"He wasn't hard on the eyes," she said.

"He obviously felt the same way about you. Let me tell you, it was a real joy to share the tent with you both."

She laughed. "Oh, come on. He was off helping the other tourists most of the time. And he slept outside on the sand, remember?"

"I've got work to do," Lovell said. It was a guillotine to the conversation. "Listen. That kid at school? He's not your problem."

She realized that she had shut her eyes, and she opened them now. "I guess not."

"I'll see you later?"

"Yeah, fine."

The hallway had been empty. On a cork board to her right had hung a row of messily painted apples with children's names. The boy would be all right, she had repeated to herself. Someone else, a teacher or an older kid or someone, would walk past and help him.

Now, as she left the school, she told herself she would drive back home, of course. Today would be a good day. It would be a good day.

Everyone had encouraged her to immerse herself more in work. Lovell, Sophie, Leah—each had a career. This was the answer. Turn your gaze outward. Busy yourself. A month or so ago, she had breezily suggested to Lovell that she open her own flower store, and he loved the idea: "Do it! Why not?" Sophie and Leah had similar reactions. This was just what they wanted for her. Her children were old enough now. Plenty of mothers with younger children had gone back to work full-time. So today she would begin. Once she got home, she would call their bank to make an appointment to discuss loans, look through the local paper for commercial rentals in town, arrange meetings with some area potters, research obtaining a license to import, check the latest regulations for organically grown flowers. She would have to make a list of all the steps to be taken—the business plan, the statement of purpose, her résumé, the bank loans, the rentals and phone calls—and of course there was the question of square footage and how large a store she would want.

She let her forehead fall onto the steering wheel. She had gotten a job delivering flowers just out of college on a whim. It had been the first job she had gotten on her own, not in her father's office, not assisting her mother at the agency. In the end, it had been a default career.

Mostly it was women who received flowers, girlfriends on Valentine's Day and anniversaries, mothers on Mother's Day, women who chatted with this twenty-two-year-old and asked whether it was safe for her to be knocking on strange doors. "I have a bodyguard in the van," she half joked with them. Sometimes she did share her route with a father of three who had recently emigrated from Haiti.

It was a surprise so many years ago to open the metal door of an apartment in Brighton and see that the strange, old-fashioned name belonged to a guy about her age. "This must be from my mother. I just graduated," he said as he took the wrapped flowers from her. Another man, smaller, with strawberry-blond hair, passed behind him. An overweight yellow lab lay on its side on a couch, two legs in the air. It could have been Hannah's own dog, Marmalade, waiting for someone to scratch her belly. The apartment was narrow and messy and she saw a hump of laundry in the middle of the hallway behind him. She smelled sweaty sneakers and lemon room deodorizer.

"These are irises. 'Butterfly Wings,'" Hannah said. "Your mother has good taste."

"Someone at the store must have helped her." He took in her face. She glanced down at the bent metal threshold, then looked back up at him and saw that his eyes were the oddest color. Brown but also gold, or a hint of green maybe. He was tall, unusually tall. He reminded her of some big, friendly kid that had just woken. She had no sense that this would be the person she would marry.

A week later she delivered a bouquet of roses to him, this time from his cousin, and the following week a basket of carnations and only then did she suspect anything. He did not deny it. "I was hoping—I mean, I thought I might see you again," he managed when she questioned him, and she smiled and said, "There are less expensive ways of getting in touch with me. The number for Fanciful Flowers is right here." She pulled a business card from an envelope attached to the plastic wrap.

Lovell invited her to dinner and she accepted. She needed a distraction after Doug. She returned to Lovell's apartment for his homemade chili and corn-bread muffins a few nights later, simple, boyish food that he seemed to think impressed her. But he did not flirt or puff himself up in the ways that so many others did with banter or feigned disinterest. Even now, so many years later, men at the bank or grocery store or in restaurants lowered their voices when they spoke to her. They punned, they joked, they rushed to pick up her fallen purse or napkin.

Over dinner, Lovell described his studies of tornadoes. The previous summer he had driven with a friend to Alberta just after "an F4" tore through Edmonton to help with cleanup and disaster relief, and he even played a small part in developing the province's emergency public warning system. He was earnest and polite and attentive; he asked about Boston University, her family, her childhood on Martha's Vineyard. She decided that she had never met anyone with this combination of innocence and intelligence. "I have ice cream too," he said after clearing the wobbly card table he and his roommate used as a dining table in the kitchen. "Neapolitan—I wasn't sure which kind you liked."

He told her about his graduate program at MIT in earth, atmospheric, and planetary sciences. "But part of me just wants to go on the road and storm-chase next semester and defer. Of course my adviser is totally against this."

She wanted to know what a tornado looked like up close, and why tornadoes and not hurricanes?

"Good question," he said. "Well, I've got this theory that hurricanes might be like these barometers of climate change.

If you look closely at sea temperatures and whatnot, you see these patterns."

She said, "Tell me more," and he replied, "Glad to."

At the end of the night, he walked her to his door and said, "Can we do this again?"

"This?"

"Dinner, talk—or whatever you'd want to do."

"Sure, I'd like that." She waited for him to close his eyes and lean down and in toward her face. But he only said, "Do you want to borrow a coat? It's cold out tonight."

Chapter 6

On Monday, Lovell let the kids decide whether to attend school for the first time since Hannah's disappearance. Both said they wanted to go back—he guessed that a sense of normalcy and routine was important for them right now. "But if you hear anything at all about Mom, can you come get me?" Janine asked.

"Me too?" Ethan added.

"Of course," Lovell answered.

A while later, he herded Janine out the door and watched as she stepped inside the bus. She half turned to wave good-bye to him, brushing her hair from her face, and then off she went to the other kids and teachers and her school. Maybe he would in fact have to go to their schools later today. What if he had to walk inside the front office and tell the secretary . . . that what?

He wandered back to the house to get Ethan breakfast—a bowl of Cheerios—and help him pack up for school. "What else do you need? What does Mom do in the morning?"

"Can I just have some milk? And a napkin? And a spoon?"

"Of course," Lovell said.

"Chocolate," Ethan commanded when Lovell handed him a glass of plain milk.

"This is better for you. You drink chocolate milk?"

"So?"

"Fine, fine." Hannah had always been a little lax about things like this. Lovell looked through the cabinet. Ripped clothing or unbrushed hair made her crazy, but, what, seventeen grams of sugar in one serving of Ovaltine, according to the label on the can, was apparently no problem.

"She gives me one squirt of whipped cream on top."

"No. Really? We even have whipped cream?"

"It's the only way I can drink it."

Lovell sighed and headed back to the refrigerator.

The two did not say much more as they downed their cereal and went to find Ethan's schoolbooks and jacket. "Are you going to get dressed?" Ethan asked him as they headed for the front door.

Lovell was still in his pajama pants and bathrobe. "I wasn't planning on it. I'm not going to my office today."

"I'll just walk myself to the bus stop."

"If you want," Lovell said, wondering when Ethan had begun to notice what anyone else was wearing.

Lovell went to open the front door. It dawned on him that he would be alone in this house today. Not one of them would be there with him. Lovell bent down and hugged Ethan before saying good-bye. "You're my best Ethan," he whispered, a silly thing he had been saying for years.

"Bye, Dad," Ethan said, and he trudged forward, his gray sweatpants bunching and pooling above his sneakers.

Lovell caught sight of a news van parked across the street again. He wondered when it had come, and why. An idea landed on him: What if he actually offered himself up to whatever reporter might be sitting inside this van, watching for him? Didn't the husband or wife in these cases usually do that? Make a plea for their spouse to return?

After the bus came and disappeared with Ethan down the street, Lovell thought more about his idea. A guy now standing outside the van adjusted what looked to be a light meter. He lifted his head and caught Lovell's eye, then leaned around the back of the van perhaps to call for someone else.

Lovell walked back inside the now empty house. He had to do this. He had to do whatever he could to help get her back. He went to the bathroom to comb his hair and check his teeth. He looked over at Hannah's bottle of lemongrass hand cream on the sink. The bathroom in her parents' brownstone where she had lived when they met had been this exotic laboratory when he first saw it, all the tall glass bottles and clay or ceramic pots of lavender and melon and cucumber and jasmine creams lining the windowsill and the sink and the side of the tub. He remembered secretly unscrewing and smelling a few. He had even tasted the huckleberry mask, though he had spat it out once his mouth registered the bitter alcohol tang.

Duncan had warned him against speaking to the press, but this would be a way to control the message right now. He tried to ignore his rapid pulse at the thought of this task that faced him.

He stepped outside, and Maya Gupta, a youngish reporter from Channel 6, was on him. "Lovell Hall!" She turned and motioned to her cameraman a few yards away. "Would you mind saying a few things?" Her round face was open and curious. She kept a respectful distance from him.

"Glad to do it," he said.

"What do you know at this point about where your wife might have gone?"

"I hardly know anything," he answered.

She asked him the sort of questions that Susan Sperck had, although with less venom, about what he knew and what the police knew.

"It seems that she might have gone to South Boston," he said. He attempted to project concern but calm—he certainly did not want to appear nervous or, worse, disingenuous. "Would you mind if I asked your viewers for help? Maybe they could call the police if any of them saw her?"

"Of course," Maya said. "Why don't you go inside and get a picture of her? We can run it with the number of the PD in town. Does that sound good?"

He nodded, relieved, and turned toward the house. A moment later he came back with a photo of Hannah wearing hot-pink gardening gloves, kneeling in front of her sunflowers in the backyard.

"So you want to look right into the lens like you're talking to a friend," she said, and although he balked at the idea of gazing directly into the eyes of all those viewers, of allowing his own eyes to be seen up close, he walked in front of the camera and moved to where he was directed to stand. "My wife, Hannah Hall, went missing last Thursday morning, October fourth," he began. He explained that she was last seen on Carson Beach in South Boston, that her bracelet had been found. "If anyone, if any of you, has seen this woman," he said as he held up the framed photo, "please contact the number of the police below."

Maya nodded, waiting for him to say more.

"And," he went on, trying to focus directly on the center of the lens now, "if you're watching this, Hannah, we miss you. Please come home."

Maya dropped the microphone and asked the cameraman, "You got that?" He nodded, and she added, "If you could get in tighter—" Her voice a degree kinder, she held the microphone forward again and asked, "Lovell, what sort of woman is Hannah? What sort of mother and wife is she? Can you give us more of a sense of her?"

He scanned the houses behind the reporter and saw a woman jogging past with her black terrier. He thought about his kids.

He thought about Hannah's face the moment after he had kicked the bed frame. He considered the holes in his alibi, which these reporters may well have seen by now. "You couldn't ask for a better woman," he began. "Or a better mom or wife."

"Can you tell us more? What are her hobbies? What does she like to do with the kids?"

The details spilled out: she had recently made each child a ceramic vase on her friend's pottery wheel and brought home rose or lavender buds every week from the shop. "She flies with her father to his hometown in the south of Ireland every year. She is a talented cook and a longtime Red Sox fan. She studied English, poetry, in college," he said, trying to ignore an image of her sulking and glaring at him from their bed that last night. These pretty details, this flattering portrait, felt like a lie. It was a lie. He hoped that the tension throughout his body was not apparent in his face. "We first met when she delivered flowers to my apartment—irises from my mother when I graduated from college."

"That's lovely," Maya said. "Thank you. Such good stuff." She flashed a look at her cameraman. He nodded once and hefted the camera from his shoulder. Maya stood for a moment, watching Lovell start to make his way toward his front door. She called to him as he reached his front stoop.

His heart beat in his neck. "Yes?"

"You take good care, all right? Be kind to yourself. Get some rest."

OVER THE NEXT couple of days, more news vans arrived and parked across the street. Lovell agreed to another interview with Maya Gupta, this time to talk about the kids and his job, Hannah's work, and more of Hannah's life. While the cameraman readied for the shoot, Maya whispered to Lovell, "You might want to go put on something a little more formal, something nicer than that sweatshirt. You need to look sympathetic, here, like you're taking this seriously." His face hot, Lovell walked back inside to find a button-down shirt and tie.

When a few more reporters arrived, he handed over shoe boxes with photographs and home videos of Hannah that he had gathered. As he stood talking to a group of newspaper reporters, he looked out and saw Susan Sperck jockeying for position behind them. "Got a minute for me?" she asked when their eyes met, and he had no choice but to nod.

She summoned her cameraman, and once they were ready, once the camera was rolling, she introduced him and reminded the viewers who he was. "I thought we could talk a little today about your marriage, Lovell."

He blinked over at the camera. "All right."

"Can you tell me how you met? How you first pursued Hannah?"

He had already told Maya about those irises, but that was for a different station. "She used to deliver flowers, and one time she showed up at my door. I had a hard time forming any words when I first saw her."

She laughed warmly. "I can only imagine." She went on to ask whether Hannah was his first girlfriend, how long they had dated, what he supposed had drawn her to him.

He had good reason to ask how these silly and vaguely offensive questions were relevant to anything, but he held back. "Yes, I guess she was my first real girlfriend. We were together for a year before we got married."

"Where did you propose, Lovell?"

While attempting to appear wistful, he described that morning in Donovan Munroe's boat, her parents only feet away, the striated cliffs of Gay Head in the distance.

The rest of the interview went on in this way. Lovell mustered whatever patience he could. "And what did she say? Do you remember her words? How long was the engagement?" *Oh God! When did you decide to do this? We haven't even talked about it. But, I think, I guess I should say yes!* "And Hannah? Did she want to wait?" *Only a few months. We didn't see the point in waiting.*

Susan's subtext barely lurked beneath the surface: whatever had Hannah seen in this particular man?

LOVELL CONSIDERED TAKING the kids somewhere else until the reporters went away, but he could not seem to wrestle this thought into any real plan. Where would they even go? He continued to stay tethered to the phone, always waiting for news that did not come, seizing up every time the phone did ring. He had given up trying to seem calm and rational in front of his kids. A full week had now passed since Hannah had gone.

On TV, her life played before them. The producers had by now edited the material into extended "in depth" stories that they ran, one with a quiet Chopin nocturne in the background. This piece had the effect of assuring that Hannah's fate would be tragic and newsworthy. The usual family photos were shown next: Hannah on snowshoes; Hannah dancing at their wedding; Hannah holding a greenish pumpkin the size of a soccer ball, Ethan by her side. Ethan, with his light eyes. Lovell stood at the corner of the living room, taking note of how they appeared on-screen, he stumbling over his scripted-sounding words, disheveled and pale in his neutral-colored tie, white button-down shirt, and tan corduroy sport jacket, an outfit that might have too obviously communicated innocence. Hannah, impossibly beautiful in those liquid fabrics, coral or lilac silk shirts or angora sweaters, with black yoga pants and a plain silver necklace, her hair in a high bun or tossed over one shoulder. She could have been a dancer, a professional ballerina. He might have been a computer geek who had stumbled into someone else's life.

An expert came on and presented a host of alarming scenarios: a carjacking in a nearby town, kidnapping, identity change, suicide.

"Turn it off," Lovell said. "I shouldn't have let you watch

any of this. Come on. Now. I'll let you know about any updates I hear." He yanked the plug from the outlet and hauled
the heavy TV upstairs to his bedroom. His face sweaty with
exertion, he leaned down and placed the thing in the corner
of his room.

Janine stood in the doorway, watching him. "I'm going next
door," she said.

"To Stephen and Jeff's?" She had spent the past few afternoons with the new neighbors, a young gay couple. Lovell had
met them only in passing. She had proudly reported back to
them that Jeff was a cellist with the Boston Symphony—and
had offered to help her with Beethoven—and Stephen an art
teacher at a private high school in Cambridge. Jeff, the "funny
one," had grown up in Montreal, and Stephen, the "quieter
one," was raised in a suburb of Paris. Apparently they watched
Bruins games and made their own sushi and had lots of friends
over all the time. Their lives, Lovell assumed, could not have
differed more from her own.

"No, to play with King and Mrs. Mekenner."

"Very funny. How about you stay here?"

"Why?"

He blinked at her. "Why not?"

"I told them I'd be there by now. Jeff's little niece Penelope
is there and I told them I'd watch her while he made dinner.
She's three. Stephen has a work meeting tonight."

"Penelope, huh?" he said. Janine's love of small children
made him unaccountably grateful. "Listen, I'm sorry you had

to see that guy on TV. They're full of it, these so-called experts. They don't know their heads from their asses."

"Language, Dad."

"Just try to forget what he said."

"If possible."

He watched her turn and leave and he drew a hand across his damp forehead. He stood there alone in his bedroom and glanced at the phone on a side table. He cracked each knuckle on his left hand.

He thought back to the last time he had seen Hannah, that morning, his idiotic hope that she would find her way back to him, that some element in that sunny, clear morning—the newness of fall, the sheer ordinariness of the day—would restore the equilibrium between them. He had hardly stopped to say good-bye to her or gauge whether she might still be upset. Anyway, he had been late for work. But the real reason, of course: he had not wanted to slide back into another ugly confrontation.

The first speed bump. When was that first jolt between them? It must have been so many years ago—maybe too long ago to be retrievable at this point.

He did remember the sense of suddenly approaching a country, some distant dreamland that he had always wanted to visit but had never been allowed to. And he grew closer and closer and finally landed, and at first he was high just being there, the strangeness and wonder of that alone, being so close to such beauty and heat and light and sweet air. He was not himself there—he was giddy and intoxicated—and his euphoria had been just what she had wanted and needed. They filled each other. They had no sense of themselves as separate entities anymore, other than as bodies who desired and were desired.

One night, he sat in her kitchen and she played Górecki for him and he watched as she sliced a nectarine for a pitcher of white sangria. Wearing only an old tank top, underwear, and an apron, she unfurled yet another story about Doug. "He actually made me chase him down a street and then locked me out of his apartment like it was some kind of game. Isn't that weird? Isn't that just warped?" She set a sliver of nectarine in her mouth.

"It's weird and warped."

She stopped chewing for a moment, and her eyes seemed to lose focus. "It keeps coming back to me, the fact that he's gone and that it's all over. I didn't know I could feel this awful in my body about a person. My heart actually hurts. My spleen hurts. I swear. And my lungs and my spine. My throat."

He wanted to comfort her but also to rid her of this pain. To cure this and any other hardship that she did and would ever have to endure. He wanted to be the one who had done this for her. He rose and went to her. He lifted her hair and kissed the nape of her neck, the top of her bare right shoulder.

This soul sickness flared up when he least expected it. But it may have become the thing against which they existed, unbeknownst to him, the thing against which they had to mobilize.

Of course time and the shelf life of desire soon interfered.

One day there was a pinch in his chest, barely detectable, when she gibed him for calling a movie a "film." A ping when she suggested that he get rid of his old Chuck Taylors and pick up a pair of "big-boy shoes."

Soon after, a late-night dinner party at Sophie's apartment, the second time he had met Sophie but his first introduction to their big but close group of friends, all couples. A photojournalist, a jewelry maker, a teacher in the Bronx, a hospice nurse. Each worked at something unique and noble. All had left academia by now and were thriving. They sat around the long table crowded with nearly empty plates and pots with crusted paella at the bottom, the remainders of eggplant and beet salads, bottles of *crianza* and *reserva*. The photojournalist, a handsome biracial guy with hair to his stomach, turned to Lovell and said, "So, Lovell, was it? You're still in school? Hannah said you're into weather?"

"Actually, climate patterns and storms. Hurricanes mostly. I'm working toward my PhD in atmospheric sciences. At MIT."

"Like I said." The guy half smiled. "Hey, you have a favorite storm? One that gets you off when you even think about it?"

He may have been mocking him, but Lovell did not care. It was theoretically an interesting question. "Lately I've been reading up on the Gulf Coast. Coastal Florida, Louisiana, New Orleans. The location of the Mississippi and the warm waters of the Gulf make it a target. Hurricane Betsy, back in 'sixty-five, just clobbered the coast. They called it Billion Dollar Betsy—it was the first hurricane to cause a billion dollars' worth of damage. It was so bad they took the name Betsy off the list of rotating names for storms. What makes it interesting is that it was really erratic and intense and no one could predict when it would hit, so nobody was prepared. In my department, a group of us are going to try to develop better predictive models, completely new ways to quickly compile the data as it's coming in from other countries."

"This isn't lecture hall," Hannah groaned, reaching for a joint that was, Lovell now saw, traveling around the room.

Sophie's boyfriend added, laughing, "Isn't Hurricane Betsy's some strip club down in Hyannis?"

Chapter 7

Nine days after Hannah's disappearance, Duncan called to tell Lovell that her wallet had been found on Carson. "No cash or credit cards, but her license was there," the detective said. "We've got a team on their way. I'd go ahead and cancel her credit cards."

Lovell dropped the briefcase he was holding on the kitchen floor. "Will do." He tried to make sense of it. She had lost her bracelet. Someone had taken her money. Someone had robbed her? But she was safe—she had to be, because the alternative? There was no alternative. Of course she was safe. Maybe she took the money and credit cards herself, left her license, decided to, what, assume another identity? He had a hard time picturing it. Still, there had to be some reason behind all of this.

Lovell decided to call Sophie. She was the last person Hannah had spoken to from home on the morning of her disappearance, according to the record on their phone.

A few days before Hannah had disappeared, there was talk of meeting up with Sophie and her husband that weekend, a barbed joke about Lovell being weirdly awkward in her presence. He could not help that Sophie intimidated him. "You have a crush on her," Hannah had said. "Yes, that's exactly it. I've always had a thing for your old college roommate," he tried, but she turned up her nose, maybe thinking, *You would never have a chance with her.*

Crush—the word itself was embarrassing and juvenile. He would have called it something else. He had, he admitted, experienced a sort of longing in Sophie's presence. After all, she was an attractive French woman, this working mother who drank grappa with abandon and went rock climbing and could speak eloquently about everything from affirmative action to national health. But he had never fantasized about her. He had never harbored hope or delusions that anything would ever happen between them.

Lovell had not talked to her since just after Hannah's disappearance, when she had come to the house with a yellow box of petits fours, a tiny candy butterfly perched on each. When Sophie answered now, he stumbled over his words. "I wondered if you would mind—I have a couple questions about a couple things. It's nothing terrible, I mean, it's all been terrible, of course." He apologized. He was only proving Hannah's theory.

"How are the children?"

"They're all right. They're doing the best they can. Some days are tougher than others, of course. I'm trying to be a good dad for them," Lovell said. He waited for her to ask about him. "At any rate, I did have a question for you. And maybe you already told the detectives . . . ?"

"Yes?"

"How did Hannah sound to you when you talked to her on the phone that morning?"

"The detective did ask me this."

"Well, did she—" he began, "did she tell you that we had an argument the night before?"

"She asked me about my work, if I'm remembering correctly. She asked me exactly what I was working on right then."

"Things have been strained," he admitted. "We've been having a tough time for a while."

"She did tell me about your fight," Sophie said.

"She did?" He wondered why this surprised him. "I'd been doing what I could to make it better. I think we both were. But she had forgotten to pay a bill." Of course this was the wrong approach. He would never convince Sophie of his logic. "I was hoping we might try counseling." What did he really hope to gain from her? Sympathy? An ally?

She did not respond.

"Hannah adores you," he said, maybe to gain whatever small amount of favor he could.

"And I adore her. If it makes you feel any better, she knew that you were trying to work on the marriage. She thought that you were—you are a good and decent person."

The words stung him. She might have at least said "husband" or even "man." "Her wallet was just found on the same beach where her bracelet turned up. That beach in South Boston."

"Oh. I guess that's good? Any news is better than no news?"

"She didn't tell you she was going there, did she?" Of course she did not. He assumed that the police would have informed him if she did.

"No, but I'm not surprised she went. We sometimes went when we were at BU. You know that beach had meaning for her."

"Meaning?"

"It was where Doug proposed."

"It was?" Lovell's face drained. Had he never asked Hannah about the proposal itself? Long ago, he had asked plenty of questions about Doug—whether they still spoke, whether he'd ever gotten reengaged or married, the sort of questions, Lovell now thought, that a jealous boyfriend might ask. "I should let you go," he said.

"Yes, my daughter just came in," Sophie said. "Please call me if you or the kids need anything. Even just a visit."

He hung up and ran his hands through his hair. Doug

Bowen had proposed at Carson Beach. Hannah had decided to drive there for whatever reason. Maybe Doug had been in Boston that day. Did he still live in Massachusetts? Lovell did not think Hannah had spoken to Doug in years, but he could not be sure.

On his computer, Lovell found a Doug Bowen living in Santa Cruz, now the manager of Shadow Noize, a small, independent record label that specialized in young rap artists in the area. It did not appear that Doug had returned to Boston since college, at least to live. He had a son, if not a wife, and a bulldog named Rex, who was shown seated on a small throne, wearing black sunglasses studded with jewels. Lovell shook his head as he scrolled down the screen.

Long ago, Hannah had shown Lovell some photographs of her and Doug standing by his surfboard on a beach, two beautiful kids clearly in love. He was tall and fit, broad through the shoulders, his chest hairless. He had fierce hazel eyes and shiny black hair, a mustache that drooped down beside his lips.

In one shot, they stood holding a surfboard between them, each with one hand, Hannah in a mustard-yellow bikini and floppy woven hat, sun-kissed and laughing, as if in an ad for beer or condoms. In the other, she had her tongue stuck in his ear as he presented his middle finger to the camera. "Charming," Lovell had said when he saw it. She had giggled and set the photos aside.

Doug was recognizable, at least somewhat, in the pictures of him online. He was still handsome, if ridiculous-looking at his age with a shaved head and thick-framed hipster glasses, his graying goatee, a small silver barbell through his right eyebrow. In another photo, he stood beside a young black rapper who smiled a mouthful of gold teeth.

THAT NIGHT, LOVELL told the kids about the wallet while they sat over dinner at McDonald's in the next town.

"What does it mean?" Ethan asked.

"I'm not sure," Lovell said.

"She got robbed," Janine said. "It's obvious."

"We don't know that," Lovell said. "This isn't some crime show or whodunit novel. If there's one thing I've learned from my work, it's that the truth is more complicated than it usually looks. All kinds of factors can come into play. Predicting something doesn't mean just jumping to the most obvious conclusion. It's always more nuanced than that."

"What the hell else would have happened?" Janine asked. "What, you think she just threw away her money and credit cards or something?"

"I wasn't saying that." Although maybe he was.

"Then what were you saying?" Ethan asked, chewing his straw. Their food had sat unwrapped and untouched on its plastic tray since they had brought it to the table.

"I don't know. I don't know what to say anymore." He sighed, overcome. Here they sat in a booth at McDonald's, speculating about what had happened to Tu.

"She was sad and she drove into Boston and then her

bracelet fell off and she got robbed and now we have no fucking idea where she is. That's what you're supposed to think, Dad."

An older couple seated side by side at the next table stared at them. They did nothing to hide the fact that they were eavesdropping. Both had gray curls that framed their faces. The man had round, thick glasses.

"Keep it down," Lovell finally said.

"I'm not yelling."

"Then watch your mouth."

Janine rolled her eyes.

"Why was she sad?" Ethan asked.

Lovell folded a napkin and set it on the tray. "She just was. How was school for you guys today?"

"She was sad because Dad got really pissed at her because he wanted her to earn more money but she didn't know how," Janine said. She finally went for her McNuggets and yanked the lid off the container of sweet and sour. She dunked a fried oval into the hot-pink sauce.

Maybe it was, in fact, that simple. Maybe in the end, the differences between him and Hannah had stemmed only from economics. He himself had had to work his way through high school and college and had amassed more student loans than he might ever be able to repay, even with his grants and scholarships. He was used to the relentless grind of paying for life. He'd not had the twenty-some years with hardly any restrictions. He and Hannah had such different lives before they met each other. They were thoroughly different people. Had she ever had to work for anything before he met her?

Of course Lovell himself had reaped the benefits of her funding. He had enjoyed three or four years of constant dining out and shopping binges and theater and vacations to the Caribbean and Switzerland, and Tunisia for their honeymoon, hypnotizing, otherworldly Tunis.

Their first night they'd sat on the roof of their hotel overlooking the souk. They sipped sugary mint tea as the call to prayer filled the city. They watched two men haggle over a piece of silk and tried to predict each other's future and the future of everyone they could think of—Lovell's parents, his brother, Hannah's sister, Sophie, her parents, even Doug, despite Lovell's obvious discomfort with that subject matter on their honeymoon.

Lovell decided to just take his and Ethan's burgers and fries home for later, and the three soon got up to leave. The couple at the next table turned their heads to watch them pass.

"Are you fucking kidding me?" Janine said as they approached a boy holding He-Man toys and smashing them together. "Skeletor? Beast Man? Look at those saggy loincloths. What kind of violent sicko guy decided to force these on little kids?"

"Keep walking," Lovell said. The couple could still hear them.

"I liked He-Man," Ethan said. "It was the secret identity of this prince, and Teela, a princess, she thought he was a total wimp and that she had to do all the work because she didn't know that he was actually He-Man."

"Sounds like you and Mom," Janine said.

"Move it," Lovell snapped.

"Take it easy," Janine said.

The couple took it all in. The man adjusted his glasses.

"Now, please. Let's go," Lovell said.

Chapter 8

It occurred to Hannah that Lovell must have been her first male friend who did not immediately try for more. When she told him this a month or so later, after one too many martinis at the Oak Bar, he replied, "Oh." He appeared relieved but then confused. "Should I apologize for not making a move?"

She smiled. "Not at all."

They began to meet at a greenhouse on Beacon Street, where sprays hissed with warm steam. Tropical plants stretched from each corner and hung from the low ceiling. A small café with just three tables was nestled in the corner. Lovell brought homework and she books of poetry, and they read and talked over tomato and mozzarella panini and cups of cappuccino. She told him about her father, originally from Ireland, a sailboat manufacturer who could be at once boisterous and aloof, her mother who had modeled as a child and had recently retired as an agent for child models. Lovell listened to everything with genuine interest. He asked to hear more about the sailboats and her mother, those child models. *What was that like for a kid? Did you ever want to do that yourself?* He looked relieved when she shook her head. Hannah eventually told him about her engagement to Doug Bowen, their summers at his parents' house at the beach outside Santa Cruz, their road trips up to Victoria and camping in Glacier, their plans to live in San Francisco after graduation and have four kids and work for Doug's uncle, who ran a liberal independent press in Oakland—and how naive she had been in the end. She told him that Doug had been seen at a Del Fuegos show with his hand down some girl's leather shorts and later in the ladies' room with some other girl who had a dog collar around her neck. Other friends came forward to Hannah with other stories, and Doug hardly tried to deny any of what he had done. "I'm so sorry, Han. I really am. But I guess it's better that you find out now than after we're married, right?" She twisted off her engagement ring and pitched it at his face.

Lovell said, "If I ever meet him, I'll pummel his ass. Seriously, I'll flatten him if you want."

"You get in a lot of fights?"

"Not really," he said. "I guess I've never even thrown a punch. Maybe I could inflict pain in some other way. Do you know anything about voodoo?" He appeared to be only partly joking.

"He's probably impervious to voodoo." She sighed. Doug was at once impervious and wide open to nearly everything in the world. His wonder, his infallibility and childlike mischief, whether in their poetry seminar or her dorm room, or on the T late at night or the Esplanade at sunrise, his insisting on reading from *Howl* while standing on a table before the students, his giving her a piggyback ride while singing "Sugar Magnolia" along the bank of the Charles—all of it was irresistible and all of it was now gone.

She and Doug used to walk by this greenhouse regularly. His apartment was a block from it, and she once suggested they stop in for a mocha. "I've got a better idea," he said, sliding his arm through hers and leading her past the café and toward his place. He whispered, "Come catch me," and moved ahead of her, walking fast and then running to his apartment building, where he let the door close behind him. She raced after him, but the building was locked and he had disappeared inside. When she rang his apartment, he did not answer. "Asshole," she said to herself, laughing. She buzzed a few other apartments until a weary-sounding woman answered. Hannah said, "I'm so sorry, but I'm here to see a friend and it seems that their buzzer might be broken." The sound of the lock releasing, the four floors of dim, creaking stairs, the pounding on Doug's door until he opened it wearing nothing but a pair of Scooby-Doo boxers, a container of ice cream in one hand. "Hannah Banana Munroe!" he said. "What brings you to this neighborhood?"

"You're an idiot," she said.

"A cute idiot."

"A cute jerk. Some poor woman in your building who sounded like she was sleeping had to buzz me in."

He shrugged and looked at her. "You've got something in your hair." He reached forward and pulled off a leaf. "You know what? I think I might love you. No, I know I do."

It was so unlike him to say this. Everything else fell away.

HANNAH THOUGHT OFTEN now about her time with Lovell in the greenhouse, the comfort of sitting across from a person with whom you could be and say anything at all. The relief of talking to a grown-up instead of a child. She was so grateful for Lovell Hall. She could come back to life now. He was a gift to her, a real ally. Those afternoons may have been their most romantic, when they were friends, before they even kissed, long before they spoke the word "love."

As she started up the car outside Ethan's school, she decided that Lovell was a decent enough person—imperfect, of course, prone to preoccupation, occasionally less than empathetic, socially clumsy. He only wanted his wife to love him.

But he nearly went at her last night. He had come close, closer than he ever had before. She had seen it, the itch just beneath his skin. A part of her could hardly blame him. She had brushed it away and made light of it in her mind later, but in the moment, she had shrunk from him, she remembered. She had been panic-stricken. And to think how safe and comfortable she had felt with him once upon a time in that greenhouse.

Chapter 9

Lovell had been planning to attend a conference in Los Angeles since long before Hannah's disappearance, but now that it approached, he figured he should bow out. Over the phone, his mother said, "You should go, even if it's just for a day or two. You've been prepping for that intensity seminar for how long?"

"All year. And last year too." The seminar would have been what he hoped was his most persuasive statement yet that as global warming intensified, so did dangerous storms. A correlation between power dissipation and sea surface temperatures was at best difficult to prove. Deterministic factors (greenhouse gases, changing natural climate cycles) and stochastic factors—chance—made weather events almost always appear random. Still, it was not so difficult to prove the *probability* of increased hurricane intensity in the coming years at least, owing to a spike in available energy from higher tropical SSTs. Of course the goal was to convince people that global warming had X effect on the earth—that if humans didn't commit to reducing greenhouse gases by X percent *today*, X cities would be destroyed, X houses would be torn apart, X people killed. Lovell had developed a new power index that could—within a reasonable margin of error—become the first tool to help quantify these things. There were few highs for him like the high of making what was assumed to be unknowable and impossible to predict considerably less so.

"You have your cell phone," his mother said. "Give the detective our number and we'll call you the minute we hear anything. You can't put your career in jeopardy, Lovell."

He protested—he would be across the country. "It's too far. It wouldn't be right. This would be the definition of leaving you and the kids in the lurch." Hannah too, wherever she was.

"Go. You have to."

In the end he changed his flight by a day so that he would be gone for only two, typed up for his mother a list of where the kids needed to be and when, and set out to call Detective Duncan. Lovell stood before the phone and considered what he was about to say: that he had chosen to leave his children and his missing wife—whose wallet had just been found, who was either walking around in Southie with no money or ID or . . . or he did not want to think of what else—in favor of his work. He set the receiver down without making the call.

HE WATCHED THE country pass beneath him on the plane: Buffalo, Cleveland, the browned mosaic of land in Iowa, while the tiny icon of an airplane inched across the screen on the back of the seat before him. The man seated next to him listened to music turned up loud in his headphones, Duke Ellington, Lovell thought—*Blues in Orbit,* was it? One of his father's favorites. He had played it the first time Lovell brought Hannah home to meet them. "Jazz orchestra," Jim Hall had declared as he went to find a certain Ellington CD, "is the only m-music that can help me unwind. There are proven c-c-correlations between a love of jazz and intelligence, a level of sophistication, that sort of thing. Did you know that Lovell used to be able to play parts of this on the p-piano when he was a kid? He was so good at the piano—I never understood when he started on the b-b-banjo later." Lovell had shrugged, embarrassed by his stuttering, usually reticent father's at- tempts to impress Hannah. As Jim went on, Lovell was sud- denly aware of the empty walls, the bare floor, the total lack of warmth or personality around them; his parents' matching plaid love seats, which had been scratched and torn by Walter, their hairless cat; the way they nattered on angrily about the condo board in their building; Hannah's hidden smile when his mother set a bowl of pea soup with an obscenely large ham hock at the center before her.

Soon after, he would wheel their suitcases onto a ferry and watch seagulls dip toward them beside the boat; he would for the first time step foot on Martha's Vineyard and take note of the wash of light reflected nearly everywhere from the ocean, the bustling, happy towns, the number of bicyclists riding alongside the cars; he would walk down a brick path lined with wildflowers toward her parents' seaside home, trying not to gawk at the vaulted wood-beam ceilings, the wall of glass that overlooked crowded Edgartown Harbor from the living room, the person—a cook? a servant?—who set plates of buttered lobster tail and pomegranate crab salad in front of them for lunch.

The man beside Lovell turned up the volume. Yes, it was Ellington.

Later, Hannah admitted that she had never much liked jazz. "It makes me physically uncomfortable," she said, and he had chided her for summarily dismissing a genre of music. "Pardon me for having an opinion," she had said. Before then, she had been the one to judge him.

THE CONFERENCE CENTER, a drafty hall bright with fluorescent lighting, smelled of insect repellent and glue. A hum of beeps and static and chatter filled the place. Lovell met up with colleagues who attended each year, and as always, they tried not to broach what they were about to discuss in detail for the next several days, but inevitably their talk about their kids and houses—as well as tentative questions about how he was holding up in the face of Hannah's disappearance—drifted to time constants and interglacials, the record heat that year, the snowfall in South Africa.

He headed across the hall to a talk about El Niño. Thirty or so people were getting settled in their seats, thirty researchers, thirty people concerned about recent anomalies in the central equatorial Pacific, where the waters ran warmer.

In the seminar room, the lights dimmed and a map of the equatorial Pacific appeared on the large white screen at the front. The presenter began to speak, and he flicked to the next map, air-flow patterns over the western Pacific, a beautiful swirl of pressure, temperature and rainfall rendered in a blotted rainbow of colors, and the next, the Atlantic, much smaller and so less capable of oscillation.

Lovell thought of Hannah's going to Carson Beach. If Lovell pictured it—if he tried to imagine that morning through her eyes, if he imagined her replaying the things that he had said to her, if he thought about her watching the kids head off for school and her facing the empty house for those few hours before she was due at the flower store, if he tried to inhabit what her thoughts might have been—then a drive to this place from her past was not implausible.

The presentation turned to the thermocline, the precise place where warm surface water met cooler, deeper water, and the changing interplay between the two.

Santa Cruz. The idea came to Lovell as if from nowhere. When was the next time he would be on the West Coast? The conference was in a different city each year. Santa Cruz had to be a reasonable drive from here.

When the seminar was finished, Lovell returned to his hotel room and found Doug Bowen's contact information through Shadow Noize. He sent off an e-mail introducing himself and suggesting they meet, as he was "in the area." Doug soon replied and agreed.

Lovell called his mother and she agreed to stay at his house an extra night. "Good luck with the seminar this afternoon," she said.

He had forgotten that it was just an hour from now. "Thanks, Mom."

"Have you seen Dot Schlage there yet?" Dot Schlage taught undergrad planetary science at MIT. She had grown up in the town next to Lovell's, and before he met Hannah, his mother used to suggest that he ask her out. Dot was nice enough and not unattractive, but she spoke so quietly he could hardly hear her most of the time. She seemed unable to look him in the eye; rather, she held her gaze at his forehead whenever the two spoke. "She's at the conference, you know."

"Mom." It felt perverse, his mother even mentioning Dot's name right now.

"I see her all the time at MIT. We have lunch sometimes. Just tell her I say hi, would you?"

• • •

THE NEXT MORNING, he checked out of his hotel and left Los Angeles as the sun rose, coral and golden, over the buildings and hills. He took a window seat near the back of the Greyhound, and as he had hardly slept the night before, he drifted off into a dreamless sleep until the stop at Santa Barbara.

The bus filled and he shifted toward the window to make room for a suntanned college-age girl who wore a bandanna over her head and carried only a ratty copy of *On the Road*. Lovell found his laptop, plugged in his headphones, and clicked on the website for Shadow Noize Records. He reread the short paragraph describing the company's early days: "We set up in the basement of the Clover Club and we just recorded live records at first. That was our thing, capturing the raw energy of live music." Beneath the words were covers of new albums released by the small label. He listened to samples of a few singles. The lyrics were stunningly violent and misogynist and materialistic. He felt old and prudish. He hoped his kids never heard this crap. He wondered if Hannah ever had.

He took off his headphones and set his head against the window. He closed his eyes and tried in vain to fall asleep again. The suntanned girl made little noises of delight as she read.

He thought back to a nor'easter years earlier. A plow had shoved an immovable wall of snow against Hannah's car outside his apartment building and the storm had shut down the nearby subway system. They walked several miles from Cleveland Circle cinema, where they had seen *The Doors,* and now, covered in wet snow themselves, they stood outside the door of his building, trying to spot where her car had once been and assessing the possibility of her going anywhere right then.

He offered his couch and she suggested his futon. "Less chance to hear Paul's trombone from your bedroom."

Maybe there is a God, he had thought.

In his room, as they changed with their backs to each other, Hannah into a shirt and sweatpants that he gave her, Lovell's face burned: what must she have thought of his *Star Wars* pillowcase, the stench from the open bag of Doritos on the floor beside his bed? She herself mentioned a rubber night guard just prescribed for bruxism—"Be glad you don't have to see me wearing it," she said generously as she fluffed Yoda and Obi-Wan beneath her head.

Lovell and Hannah soon lay on their backs, and he watched the white dust sink and dance past the streetlights outside.

She finally broke the silence: "We are in bed together. I'm wearing your old undershirt. Say something."

I love you, he thought. "Something."

"Ask me a question. Anything you want."

He scrambled to think of something daring, the sort of question that she might ask. "What is your biggest regret in life?" he thought to say. "What are you the most proud of?"

She answered and then countered easily: "Describe your first time having sex." "What's the angriest you've ever been?" "Have you ever been arrested?" His answers were embarrassingly tame next to hers. She regretted turning down a romantic advance from "a very well-known actor who shall remain nameless" when he was in Boston a few years ago. She was proud that she and Doug had surfed some deathly wave in Oahu. She had lost her virginity on her father's boat when she was fourteen to a twenty-year-old neighbor, home from college at the time; she'd had a threesome on a beach in North Carolina. In turn, Lovell regretted never having known his mother's parents, who had her when they were older and died before Lovell was born. He was proud that he was on his way to a PhD. He had made love with three women before now, each one in his dorm room. The angriest? "Probably when you told me about Doug."

"That was *your* angriest?" She smiled and brushed a spot of lint from his cheek. "You're sweet. You're just *you*," she said. She held her finger against his face for a brief moment before pulling back.

He made himself edge forward and say, "Can I?"

She nodded. He took her face in his hands—the face he had pined for all these months. Hannah Munroe's face. He pushed his lips against hers, and spinning inside, weightless, he kissed her. They kissed each other.

After, she buried her face in her hands.

"You all right?" he asked.

She shrugged and wiped her eyes. "I'm fine. This is good— you are good."

Was he her first since Doug? "Should we stop? Did I do something that you didn't want to?"

"No, no. Please, you're fine. This is fine. Just don't go anywhere."

"I won't," he said, reaching for a hair that clung to her eyelashes. "I'm right here."

OVER NINE HOURS after he had left Los Angeles, the bus pulled into the station in Santa Cruz. Lovell hauled his bags from the metal rack above him, stepped down the cramped aisle and steep stairs, and stood blinking in the hazy sunlight of the afternoon. A few others disembarked behind him, and he moved to the side and glanced at his watch—he had just enough time to check into the motel, a block away from here, and walk to meet Doug.

Rocco's Diner, a place Doug had suggested, was a steel double-wide with a scene of a nearly 3-D psychedelic goddess Roller Derby air-painted across its front. Lovell realized he had been standing in the parking lot, staring at the tacky mural for minutes now, the buxom, winged women gliding toward him through a purple rainbow and haloed black sun.

The diner was nearly empty. A couple of teenagers sat chattering loudly in a booth. And there at another torn booth, by the restroom, facing Lovell, sat a bald man with a black-and-gray goatee and a pierced eyebrow, a mug in his hands as he chatted with a waitress who had a short Mohawk. "Doug?" Lovell said from behind the waitress.

"My brother," Doug said, standing to hug him as if he had

known him for years. He muscled Lovell past the waitress and into his arms for a powerful hug. "How you holding up?" he said.

"I don't know," Lovell said as he lowered himself into the booth. He edged past a rip on the seat where white fluff burst from the vinyl. "Thanks for agreeing to meet."

"No need to thank me."

Lovell reminded Doug that it had been twenty days, three weeks, since Hannah had disappeared. "Unbelievable."

"I bet."

For some reason he said, "People recognize me from the news."

"I'm sure it's totally fucked with your mind." Doug began to flick at his eyebrow ring.

Lovell tried not to watch. He kept his eyes on the chipped laminate tabletop and thought about the best way to respond.

"I've been lucky," Doug said. "Never had to deal with anything like that."

"Well, you do—you did know her."

Doug laughed. "I stand corrected. You have kids? They OK?"

Lovell wondered how much—or how little—Doug already knew from the news or mutual friends. Or from Hannah herself? "We have a son and a daughter. Ethan and Janine."

"Nice. I have a boy, five. D. J., Doug Junior. Not my idea, mind you, his name. I wanted strong and easy, maybe Max or

Nick." The waitress returned to bring coffee and water and take their orders, and when she left, he continued. "I never got married." At last he dropped his finger from his eyebrow.

"I'm sure you know that I met Hannah just after you two, after you—"

"I was glad she found someone to take care of her." Doug squinted at Lovell. "I didn't deserve her. I loved her, I really did. We were wild about each other, but I sure didn't deserve her."

"Well, it's history, I guess. Water under the bridge." Lovell was thankful for clichés. This was no time for a heartfelt connection. The transfer of information—that was all he needed.

"What's it been, seventeen years now since me and her? We're getting to be old men, brother."

Lovell tried to sound casual. "You ever, you know, see her over the years?"

"I been out here for fifteen years now."

Why would this person be honest? What would he have to gain? "I mean, OK, I'll be specific. You weren't in Boston on that day. You didn't see her the day she went missing?"

Doug's pale eyes widened. "I haven't seen Hannah Munroe since the time she nearly took out my tooth with the engagement ring that I got her."

His use of her maiden name, the near laugh as he spoke. Lovell's temperature spiked. "Your proposal, I mean, on the beach. You have to know that's where her wallet and a bracelet were found."

Doug took a long swig of his orange juice and smacked his lips. "No shit. Really?" He ran his hands gently over his bald head as if it were a baby. "That's right. Carson, was it?"

Lovell reached for his coffee. He had of course hoped to manufacture a reason for Hannah to drive to Carson that day—a reason other than himself. Someone to help shoulder the blame. "Something like this can really make you crazy."

Doug nodded.

The waitress came back with their plates of food, and it occurred to Lovell that a quick coffee somewhere might have been a better idea. A towering club sandwich sat before him, a heap of curly fries to the side.

"So," Doug said, reaching for his avocado wrap, "you like LA?"

"I didn't get to see much of it," Lovell replied. He tried to chat lightly about his work and the conference. He told him about the intensity seminar and the crowd that it had drawn. "This power index that I've been working on is kind of a big deal—" Lovell said. As he went on, he took in Doug's aging but boyish face and gray-gold eyes. Doug popped a bite into his mouth and half smiled at Lovell—an impish, disarming smile. What would it be like to have such a smile? To be charming without having to say a thing? Lovell told him about his column at *Weather*. "I probably get ten letters a week about it. Too many to answer, really." Doug nodded as he listened, interjecting "Nice" or "Good for you." He was, of course, just humoring him.

Lovell took a few bites of his sandwich, skipped his luke-warm coffee, and waited for Doug to finish his wrap. When he finally did, he reached into his back pocket for his torn leather wallet and slid a faded credit card from one of its pockets. "My treat. Least I can do, right?" Doug said. He stood and reached out a tattooed hand and said, "I gotta talk to her for a sec," gesturing toward the waitress. "So I'm gonna say good-bye." He again looped an arm around Lovell's back and folded him into his chest. "Keep on keeping on, OK? You do what you have to do. And if you ever need anything from me, you've got my info."

Lovell eased away. "Sure, all right. Thanks." He strode to the door and let it bang shut behind him.

He walked at a brisk clip across the lot and back toward the motel, just a few minutes away, trying to convince himself that coming here had not been an enormous waste of time.

His room reeked of cigarette smoke and rot, some kind of mold or something. He hadn't noticed it so much earlier. He heard a woman hacking in the next room, a man somewhere talking, and the buzz of a radio or TV. He took a seat on a heavy wooden chair in the corner just as the phone rang. It was his mother, saying that he should come home as soon as he could. "That detective called. He said he had no idea that you were in LA. He needs you to go down to the station and he wouldn't tell me why."

Chapter 10

Once back from Ethan's school, Hannah headed to the kitchen and scrubbed the breakfast dishes. She wandered upstairs and into her bedroom, where she drew the shades and tidied the bed and fluffed the pillows in an effort to make the room feel less like a war zone. She stepped into the bathroom. It smelled of perfume still, the perfume that Sophie had brought her from Paris and that Lovell had now gone and trashed. At least he had thought to clean it up. At least the bathroom would smell like Coco for another day or so. Then she would stop and notice that the scent had faded and remember that she could not afford to buy any more. She couldn't stand to be in this room any longer. She couldn't stand this rage.

She closed the door behind her and walked down the hallway to neaten up the kids' bedrooms. She sat on Ethan's bed and smoothed his soccer-ball quilt around her. She set his ko-ala beside his pillow. On his first day of preschool, she had inhaled those few hours to herself. It had seemed like a decade since she'd had a moment alone. She had stretched out on an Adirondack chair in the backyard and noticed the clouds as if for the first time, gauzy like spun sugar low in the sky. She had flipped through a magazine and breathed in each perfume ad—pungent musk, lilac and lavender, black cherry—and then had called Sophie to say hello. Having nothing to report had been a luxury.

She walked downstairs to the kitchen now. She picked up the phone and dialed Sophie's number at work. "I thought I'd just call to say hi like I used to," Hannah said.

"Oh. Is everything all right?"

"Sure. What are you doing right now?"

"Specs for a print ad," she said. She was single-handedly overseeing ad campaigns for Blue Cross and Blue Shield and for the Gap. "Are you really OK?"

"Absolutely. Let's get together soon."

"We have plans, all of us, for this weekend, no?" Sophie asked.

Hannah had meant that just the two of them should go somewhere they might have gone before having kids—see an old movie at the Brattle or wander around a used-book store. "I guess so. I forgot."

"We'll think of something fabulous."

"We will," Hannah said. "We got into it again last night,

me and Lovell." She considered telling Sophie that she thought Lovell had a crush on her.

"Oh?"

"You have to work. I should let you go."

"I'll call you on my way home later. I'll call you as soon as I leave the office. You'll tell me then?"

"Sure," Hannah said.

But what would be the point of rehashing it all? What would that change? This was her life, this was her marriage. No one had forced her into it.

Lovell had stunned her by proposing on her father's boat with her parents looking on. He had never mentioned marriage before. She could not exactly say no. Nor did she want to.

Later, when he suggested a short engagement, maybe a wedding on the Vineyard, nothing elaborate, just a meaningful gathering of their favorite people, Hannah had agreed. Too much time and she might change her mind. She was ready to be married. She wanted to be done with all the heartbreak that happened when you weren't married.

"We don't really talk anymore," she had said to Lovell about two weeks ago. God, she had become a broken record with him.

"Sure we do."

"Not really."

He looked over at her from his laptop, the comforter tented over his legs.

"OK," he said. "So, I've got this idea to write up these

scenarios, these stories about people and how we harm the climate without realizing it."

"Yeah?"

"I could write a monthly column for the magazine. I'd trace one atom as it travels. The atom would be like the—I don't know—the protagonist or antagonist, depending on what happens, and in each column, I'd set out this different scenario."

She wondered how such a thing as an atom—anything other than a person, really—could be made a compelling protagonist. But she knew better than to question his approach to his work. The few times she had, he had gently shut her down. What did she know about the movement of atoms or the physics of climate change?

"I could write about forest growth or I could set it in different countries—China, all the pollution. And I'd show people exactly how the gas that they buy or their TV or whatever—I'd show exactly what impact these things have on the earth. How one molecule of carbon actually moves and where it goes once it's emitted, what happens to it and everything around it. It's not hurricanes, it's not what ME has me doing, but that's the point. Try something different, maybe for the layperson rather than just the people who already know this stuff. I think I'll put some feelers out. I can e-mail my editor, see what he thinks about it." He finally turned back to his computer. "I have so much work to finish tonight."

Talk, she nearly said. *Not a talk. I did not ask for that.*

She still had time before work. She could go food shopping,

though there was enough in the refrigerator to last the next several days. She could fold the kids' laundry and get the car washed and return some library books. She had enough time for a nap, but then she would have to summon the energy to extricate herself from the warm bed.

Or she could do something else. She could do something that she had never done—drive to a part of town where she had never been, pretend to be someone that she was not. A lifetime ago, she and Doug used to close their eyes and set one fingertip on a map of Massachusetts, some town, ideally a place where they had never been. They would gather the map and her keys and, on the way, choose identities for each other. Once, at a beachside diner in Revere, she and Doug pretended to be a movie star and an army sergeant visiting from Texas.

She could, if nothing else, go for a drive. Maybe Carson Beach for a quick walk. She had not been in so long—since she had gotten engaged to Doug. Was that the last time? She had been molecularly a different person, giddy and hopeful. "I have the craziest idea," he had said. "Let's get married."

"What?" she said. They were twenty-one. "We're too young."

"You want to wait until we're too old?"

She nearly jumped up and yelled to the heavens, but she knew better. "Where's my ring?"

He glanced around and reached for a string of dried seaweed on the sand. "I'll make you one," he said, trying to twist the thing into a circle, but the seaweed was too dry and broke in half. Finally he knelt down on the sand and leaned his head against her legs, not saying a thing. He reached for her hand and set the piece of seaweed in her palm.

Was this even a bona fide proposal? "Doug?"

He looked up at her with those goddamned eyes that turned her to soup. His reckless impulsivity, his sudden chivalry with pretty girls, his tendency to forget bills—he would outgrow all of that. Everyone did at some point.

"Let's do it," she said.

Chapter 11

When Lovell returned Bob Duncan's call, the man spoke somberly. "You should have told us you were leaving the state."

"'Leaving the state?'"

"When are you coming back?"

Lovell explained that he would return the next afternoon. "As soon as my plane lands, as soon as I can, I'll get in my car and drive directly to the station. Can you tell me what's going on there?"

"To be honest, I'd rather talk to you in person." The man sneezed into the phone, and Lovell jolted.

"I'm sorry," Lovell said before he hung up. "I'm sorry I didn't let you know where I was."

"It was a strange decision," Duncan said. "At any rate, I'll see you tomorrow."

The traffic on the drive to the airport in San Francisco, the wait at the gate, the delay before the plane took off, the flight itself, the wait to get off the plane while the other passengers reached for their overhead baggage and zipped up their jackets and cleaned off their seats and wriggled their way down the narrow aisle—everything moved with infuriating sluggishness in front of him.

On the drive out of Boston, he thought of one of their earliest arguments, the morning after a party at her parents' house on the Vineyard. He had sneaked into her bedroom before the sun rose. He watched her as she slept tucked into herself, her rosy mouth open as she breathed. The bed was positioned alongside a bay window that looked out over the Atlantic, glittering with the waning moonlight. After she woke, she sat up in bed and gave him a kiss on his arm. She began to discuss her family's behavior the previous night: her mother's tendency to subtly compete with her sister; her name-dropping cousin who worked in a Manhattan law firm; her sister's resentment of their father, who showed no interest in Leah's academic successes. Lovell tried to hide a yawn and began to gently wrestle Hannah back to bed, but she resisted. "Did you notice any of that?" she asked. "Not really," he admitted. "Doesn't it interest you at all?" she said.

Lovell, his hand around her naked thigh, finally said, "I don't know. I guess all families are weird. Oh, and you should have prepared me for your father's *boat,* which, by the way, is really a yacht. You could fund a nation with that thing."

She pulled away. "You can't stand this, just sitting here and talking. You are happier screwing or just sitting across from me, silent, than actually engaging in any conversation." She may have had a point; he loved little more than lounging on his couch with her, both of them lost in a book or a movie. "Sue me for just loving to *be* with you," he finally said. And what could she say to that?

A thought landed on him like a tentative moth: maybe they should never have gotten married.

But then another thought: Tunisia. It stood behind them like a lighthouse in a forest. Nothing like what a honeymoon should be. No starry-eyed murmurings while lying in bed together. No marathon sessions of lovemaking, just a moment of rescue, or near heroism, and the grateful look on her face, the belief that they had absolutely done the right thing in coming together.

The parking lot at the police station was almost full, and Lovell sped past the other cars, drumming the heel of his palm against the steering wheel. He finally found a spot on the street adjacent to the station and hurried inside.

Bob Duncan's office door was closed, so Lovell knocked. As he waited, he began to wonder why he had been so anxious to get here. What news—what good news—could there be at this point?

Duncan pulled open the door and led him into the office.

"I'll get right to it. The guys found fingernail marks on a pier at Carson."

"Fingernail marks? Do you know they're even hers?" This was Hannah they were talking about. Tu. This was his wife.

"I want you to think back hard now and make sure there's nothing you might have forgotten to tell me. No store she once went to near Carson, no old friend who'd just moved there. Anything at all you can think of that might help us here?" he asked. "Oh, and we got the match this morning. So yes, the fingernail marks were hers."

"But—oh." Lovell took a seat. She could have been trying to etch her initials into the pier. It was just the sort of thing she would do.

"You can't think of anything?" Duncan said, incredulous. "Why do you think she went all the way into Boston when she had to go to work that morning?"

"Could she have been carjacked or kidnapped or something?"

"We don't know yet. We haven't found her car. But she did make that phone call to the girl at the flower store. The call was traced to Boston. The girl said Hannah didn't sound strange or anything, that she was convincing when she said that your daughter was home sick. My guess is that Hannah drove in and that no one took her to Boston."

"Ok."

"But if there was some reason for her to go there, if there's even the smallest thing you can think of—and it might seem like nothing to you—we need anything we can get at this point. Somewhere she meant to be going, someone who might have seen her."

"I don't have a clue about why she would have gone there specifically," Lovell said. He assumed that by now Duncan knew about Doug Bowen and his proposal on Carson Beach. Lovell considered the possibility that Duncan already knew about the fight the evening before, that Janine or someone else, maybe Sophie, had told him. And that the man was testing him right now. Duncan had wanted to get him here in person, to give him the news about the fingernail marks so that he could see the reaction on Lovell's face. Lovell had no choice but to tell him everything. His stomach lurched as he began.

"OK, hold on," Duncan said. "Have you told anyone else about this yet?"

"No," Lovell said. "I should have. I knew it wouldn't look good, that it, I mean, it might be taken a certain way, but now that all this is happening, I guess I figured she'd be back now and that it wouldn't matter so much. I could take a lie-detector test."

"They're nightmares in court. Judges don't like them. But wait—slow down. Let me ask you some things. Did you threaten her?" Duncan asked. "Did it get physical?"

"I didn't hit her or anything."

"OK. Any reason she would have felt unsafe?"

"Well, infinitely pissed off at me. It wasn't my best night,"

he said. "But I don't think, I mean, probably not *unsafe.*"
Maybe Duncan had not, in fact, known.

"You ever hit her? You ever push her around or anything
else like that? Get a little too rough?"

"No," Lovell said, relieved to be able to answer this question clearly.

"She ever disappear before?"

"Once, just for the night," Lovell explained, but he told the
detective that she had returned early the next morning.

And finally: "You think she was depressed?"

"Possibly."

"All right. These are standard questions that I have to
ask." The detective cleared his throat. "Could she have been
suicidal?"

"No, I don't think so," Lovell said. "I mean, I guess I can't
say for sure. She wasn't happy."

"Did she ever talk about hurting herself?"

"No."

"You sure?"

"Sometimes she took Sominex to help her sleep. A year ago,
she couldn't sleep for weeks, and one night she took maybe
four or five."

"You'd need to take more than that to do any harm."

"That last night she was miserable." Lovell wrapped one
hand around his other. "But I think she just, that she couldn't,
you know, stand *me.*"

"All right," Duncan said.

"All right?"

That was it? The detective began walking him toward the door. "I'll be in touch when I hear anything more."

Lovell wanted to ask the man what he thought now. What was his opinion of Lovell now? Had he gained anything from being honest? Even if it was a little too late in the game? Duncan just said good-bye, took a step back into his office, and closed his door.

Lovell made his way outside and back to his car. The kids were at home, waiting for him. Apparently, Janine had protested his staying away an extra night, which was understandable.

There was no good reason to tell them about the fingernail marks. It was the sort of news that implied more than it told, and it would upset them. It would scare them. Janine's mind would rush to horrible places. If they read about it in the newspaper or saw it on TV, then he would talk it over with them. He would remind them that they didn't have the full picture yet, that they should hold out hope until they had every piece of information they could get. They owed Hannah this much.

As he drove home, he thought more about this latest news. She was angry at him; she was angry at herself. She sat there on the beach, raging at him and, without even noticing that she was doing so, scratching deep marks into the wood. It was not all that far fetched. The things he had said to her that night. She must have been livid.

Chapter 12

Hannah grabbed her purse and locked the door behind her. Autumn pollen caked the windshield of the car. She turned on the wipers and the wiper fluid. She backed her car out toward the street and narrowly missed the milk truck. The driver blasted her horn and gave Hannah the finger. Shaken, Hannah inched down the street, her foot on the brake as she approached the stop sign at the corner of the Sullivans' property and then the overgrown willow that spilled toward the street and brushed her windshield as she passed. She stopped beneath the tree and watched the wipers scrape the thick dust back and forth in a choppy rhythm and ensnarl one of the wispy branches, tearing it from the tree. She shifted to park, switched off the wipers, stepped out of the car, and yanked at the branch now braided around the torn rubber blade. She removed the blade from its rusted frame and picked at the gnarled stem that wove taut around it. She glanced over at the weeping willow, a mass of downward movement. It was a gorgeous tree. She wound the branch into a loose reel and set it on her backseat. Maybe she could replant part of it later in her backyard.

She drove toward town, past the Victorians with their broad porches and window boxes ("Mums, mums, and more mums," she often complained), the rhododendrons bunched in front, the brick library, a group of preschoolers clutching a red rope and toddling down the sidewalk as they did each day. They looked at their feet, the sky, the cars—these sweet, jittery little people. She rarely, if ever, saw preschoolers or toddlers anymore. She counted the years since Ethan had been a toddler: five, almost six. Hannah had married and had her children, and this time now was shaped only by the maintenance of those things that had come before.

Ten years ago, when she and Lovell had been visiting her parents, she had surprised him with cross-country skiing on the beach during a blizzard. She had filled a thermos with bourbon. She had blindfolded him—and he protested and squirmed. He could hardly sit still during the short drive to Lambert's Cove. "I've never liked surprises," he griped, and she said, "Who doesn't like surprises?" She refused to take off his blindfold until she had walked him up the snowy dune and onto the untouched beach, now a rumpled expanse of white. When she finally loosened the knot of the bandanna behind his head, he blinked at all that was around them, and said, "What is this?"

She gestured beside them to the skis and poles that she had dragged along.

"No. It's minus twenty degrees, and these winds are blowing vertically." The surf spat up onto the snow.

"Jesus, live a little," she said.

"All right, all right." He pulled the zipper on his winter jacket up to his chin. "I'm sorry," he said.

"You can be such an old man." What had once been comforting had become restrictive, his unwavering logic and good sense. She tried to articulate this to him, to talk above the din of the wind and waves, her boots dug into a bowl of snow, to define this shrinking air inside her as a problem for both of them, but the shrillness and banality of her own loud words rang in her ears: *I want more. I want. I want.* Maybe she should no longer expect spontaneity. Was it unseemly at her age, a woman with a child and a husband and a home in a nice suburb, to try to get her husband drunk on Jim Beam and fuck him by the ocean in the middle of winter? "I sound like a shrew," she said at last.

He pressed his mouth against her ear so that he would be heard. "Sometimes I can't tell whether you are arguing with me or with yourself." He tried to rekindle her mood. "Come on, let's just do this." They got their boots and skis on, their scarves wound tight. They glided a length of the beach, up and down the gradual slopes. She maintained a wide lead at first, but then he caught up and they skied side by side for a while. "This is nice," he called to her.

When the beach grew narrower, she motioned for them to stop and she collapsed through a crunchy layer of snow. She lifted the thermos of liquor from her backpack and poured him a shot. She watched him pinch his eyes shut as he made himself down the bourbon in two pained gulps. She poured another small cupful, and they sat on the beach, huddled together in the icy air, and kissed gently for a moment, he apologetically, she dutifully. "I'm glad you got me out here," he tried, and she nodded, if nothing else appreciative of his lie.

She was meant to exude calmness and control and, more than anything, stasis. She was meant to react to everyone else in a predictable way, never to provoke, never to incite. Women pretended that everything had changed over the years. Hannah thought of her mother. Did she ever have these sorts of thoughts? Lydia Munroe had little tolerance for self-questioning and indecision. She had set up the life she had wanted, and that was that. She had a clear image of the women she expected her daughters to become: emotionally strong, sufficiently pious, attractive women who were self-possessed and in control of every aspect of their days. Each night she timed the girls when they brushed their teeth (five minutes according to an egg timer kept on a shelf above the toilet) and took baths (no less than thirty minutes). "She was this walking contradiction in her silk paisley shift with her hair in a neat bun on top of her head," Hannah told Lovell soon after their engagement. They had met Leah for dinner in Chinatown and sat in a booth over green tea and Yu Shiang shrimp. "She'd hold court from the head of the kitchen table. Remember?" she asked Leah. "She'd wave her paperback copy of *The Feminine Mystique* in one hand and a Virginia Slim in the other. And then she went to church each Sunday." Rennie, the housekeeper, cooked dinner most nights, but Lydia always chose the menu.

Lydia demonstrated to the girls the privileges that came from stealthily but firmly maintaining household control. She taught them to simultaneously project fragility and strength, accessibility and mystery. She showed them how to walk a runway: head up, shoulders back, hands planted on hips. She taught them the various voices that a girl must use: the restaurant voice ("gentle but audible"); the department store and bank voice ("similar to your restaurant voice, but with more presence"); and the dreaded voice to be used in the presence of boys ("Quiet, with a hint of bewilderment. But at the same time, assurance—assurance is everything. Assurance, mystery, even danger"). Hannah and Leah had snickered across the booth from each other at this last word.

When Hannah was seven or eight, Lydia coaxed her to drop a live lobster into an iron pot full of boiling water, despite her abject refusal. "Boys love a girl with some savagery, but not too much. Never too much," she said. "Now, come on. It's your father's birthday and he is waiting for his dinner."

Leah set down her tea. "Dad, on the other hand, is the most

harmless, obedient man you'll meet," she said, reaching for more rice.

"He's got his opinions," Hannah said.

"Maybe. Still, Mom thought that the woman always had to wear the pants. I guess she was ahead of her time in some ways."

"Well, she worried for us," Hannah said. "She still does." She turned to Lovell. "I think she is secretly terrified that the bottom will fall out. Don't forget that her own mother had two husbands leave her. Mom's got this secret fear that if you don't control your life, if you don't control your man, he will eventually destroy you."

Leah said, "We love to analyze our mother."

"Ah," he said. He moved his eyes from one face to the other, probably confused by this family that was so different from his own.

Hannah drove on past the stark white church, the small ranch houses farther apart, the trees that split the sunlight, those trees that made the town seem rural and tucked in. Insular. The other week, she had half-jokingly suggested to Lovell that they pick up and move to Boston or even New York, or why not another country, and he had said, "Sure, the kids would love that—leaving their schools and all their friends. Mass Environmental too, right?"

She stayed to the outside of the rotary and passed the prison and the stout farm stands with their pumpkins and gourds all laid out in the sun and eventually the turnoff for Walden Pond.

On the highway to Boston—that wide, flat road, the sky uninterrupted—cars and minivans surrounded her, so many cars and strangers right beside and behind and in front of her. Any one of them could jerk their steering wheel—or she could, just like that, in less than a second.

She entered Fresh Pond, the switchback road between those proud old houses. On Storrow Drive, cars flew through the quick turns as if on a racetrack, and her knuckles tight on the steering wheel, she took the Copley Square exit, which led her inside the motor of the city, businesspeople rushing across streets, clothes stores, bookstores, banks and more banks, cabs, tourist buses meant to look like ducks filled with mothers and fathers and kids quacking at the pedestrians, and the park, more silky, drooping willows, those poignant trees, the swan boats now tied together for the season. The empty boats floated on the water, drifting apart, then knocking back together.

She turned and drove through Chinatown, passed its glossy red facades, the stores and sidewalks throbbing with people, the shiny chickens upside down in the windows. As a child she had once found a dead frog on the seat of her bicycle, the still little thing belly-up to the sun, its rubbery arms and legs splayed out. Leah had left it there. Hannah hollered for her mother. "It's just a frog," Leah said, laughing, but Hannah sprinted away down the street, her heart in her stomach. It hadn't gotten any easier over the years, the sight of a dead animal. She had dropped that lobster into the bubbling pot and slammed on the cover, raced barefoot down the hallway and into the coat closet. She had wedged herself between the winter jackets and snow pants, hiding until her father came to find her, her kind, generous father, who said, "I couldn't do that as a kid either, sweetie." She didn't know anyone else as shaken by the sight of something dead. No one else had had to be exempted from dissecting frogs and fetal pigs in middle school. She had never gone to an open-casket funeral, even her grandparents'. "It's odd, I know," she explained to Lovell soon after they met, and he seemed more bemused than anything else. "You're cute. I loved dissection," he admitted. "Does that make *me* odd?"

She fixed her gaze on the rear window of the car ahead of her until she left Chinatown. She drove above the lumpy black water, past the Children's museum, the Westin, and onto the surprisingly clean and quiet streets of Southie. Hadn't it been here where, just last week, that elderly woman had been robbed and then beheaded? Or was it Roxbury? But what a naive suburbanite she was—it could have happened in Beacon Hill, for all she remembered.

The daylight glittered around her, and a crumpled paper bag blew past her windshield. She tried to ignore a rising disquiet. If she turned the car around now, she might be only twenty minutes or so late for work, and if she hit traffic, well, no one would mind all that much. She could tell them Janine was home sick, or that Ethan was, or anything, really.

At last she approached the beach and its long, narrow parking lot. Carson itself had been cleaned up, the water now devoid of garbage and broken old boats bobbing on the tide.

She sat for a while facing the dark mirror that led to the sky and the tall grass and thought that it was pretty and seemed far from home here. If she turned her face from the buildings behind her, she could have been anywhere—Seattle or Savannah, Portugal or France, Duncannon Beach near her father's childhood home or even dreamy La Concha in San Sebastián, where she had gone with her family when she was fifteen.

Chapter 13

Janine came home one afternoon bald, only a shadow of stubble across her head. When Lovell first saw her as she walked into the kitchen, he dropped the glass plate he was holding. "Hair," was all he could say.

"Yes," she said. "It's no longer with us."

He could see the contours of her skull and the dark raised birthmark at her hairline. "You thought about this first?" He reached for the shards of glass on the floor. He had gotten back from the West Coast a few days ago.

"How about 'It looks good.' How about 'That was so brave of you, Janine.'"

"OK, OK, give me a second."

"Go ahead and say it: I don't conform to your ideas of what a girl should look like, and that scares the shit out of you."

"Oh, please, give me a break," he said. "It's not like you went out and just bought a boy's sweater or something." It occurred to him that Hannah had disappeared a month ago today. "Is this some sort of reaction to what's happening with Mom?" In movies, at least, girls and women so often shaved their heads—or at least cut their hair—when they were angry or sad.

"You can sound like a total dick when you want to."

"Janine." She looked just awful. Was that sexist to think? He couldn't help it. In her gray sweatshirt and old jeans, she looked like one of those hostile boys who sat on the curb outside the 7-Eleven every day.

"Stop staring at me like I'm some freak."

"I'm staring at you because you are my daughter and you don't look like you right now. I'm trying to get used to what you do look like."

Ethan appeared in the doorway. "What happened to you?" he asked.

"Take a good look, Eth," Janine said. "Get used to it."

He glanced over at Lovell, confused.

"Janine Ruby Hall," Lovell said.

"What?"

He could only think to find the dustpan and broom and clean up the pieces of glass scattered around him.

"Can I touch it?" Ethan asked her.

Janine bent over so that he could run his fingers across the top of her head. "That is sick."

"He means he likes it," she said to Lovell.

"I know what he means," Lovell said, although he hadn't been so sure.

"Can I do that to my hair?" Ethan asked.

Lovell said, "No." He almost asked both of them, *What would your mother say right now?* But he thought better of it and left the kitchen.

In the living room, he ran his eyes past the framed pictures on the mantel. Since Hannah had disappeared, he had avoided looking directly at the one photograph of her, that picture of her kneeling in the garden. Nearly all the stations teased the story with this photograph. It was the first one that he gave them.

Janine had taken the picture. She'd had to write an essay for school about someone she admired. Lovell had been a little surprised that she had chosen Hannah, with all her questions about his work and weather at the time. But Janine had also studied Hannah as she blow-dried her hair in the mornings and dabbed makeup on her face, and asked her why. Why did she think she needed it? *How do you shave your legs, how did you meet Dad, how much do you love him? How much do you love me? Because I love you so much, Mom, more than music, more than Ethan.* Lovell had melted, listening from the next room. Hannah had certainly earned these moments. She was still toilet training Ethan then, still scrubbing his accidents from the carpet in the hallway, still cooking three different meals for them at dinner, getting up each time Ethan had his night terrors and then finally just past dawn, when the boy typically woke for the day—and Lovell tried to when he could, but without his sleep he was hopeless and could hardly be expected to work the next day. He let her sleep in sometimes, when he could, on weekends. Once, he brought her breakfast in bed on her birthday. But these things that Janine said—"I love you to infinity"—these were the real prizes, and it was good to see Hannah flash a secret smile at him and finally savor the feeling of being adored.

And then, almost overnight, Janine could hardly tolerate her mother anymore.

The picture—Hannah's widemouthed laugh, her abandon—gave the sense that you and Hannah were in on some hilarious secret. What had Janine said the moment before the shutter clicked? Behind her, a row of sunflowers tilted back and faced the sky. He reached for the frame. Tu. Smiling with her flowers maybe five years ago. Hannah's face, her long hair, those dimples.

Lovell held the photo in one hand as he tidied some books on the coffee table and moved Ethan's sneakers to the bottom of the stairs. At least Hannah had Ethan. At least one kid still looked up to her. Lovell finally left the photo on the side table near the front door, where it would be seen each time someone stepped inside.

Janine appeared right behind him. "I heard about the scratch marks, you know."

He froze. "The marks on the pier?"

"What, did you think we wouldn't find out?"

"I don't know what I'm thinking anymore. I guess I was trying to protect you."

"Well, you should stop doing that." Her disdain for him was even more apparent without any hair to obscure it.

"We are not in some TV show here. This is real life. This is your mother. You're allowed to be sad sometimes. You don't always have to be this tower of strength, this warrior princess, you know?"

"*Warrior Princess?*" she snorted. "What, like Xena? I don't remember her ever shaving her fucking head."

"You know what I goddamned mean. Instead of being pissed off at me, maybe stop and have a good cry once in a while." He looked over at her. He himself had yet to cry in front of them. Had he ever?

"Don't tell me what to feel," she said, but something in her face sank a little.

"Listen," he began. "There could be plenty of explanations for those marks."

"Right."

"We don't know everything yet. We don't. It makes no sense to panic before we have all the answers."

"I so disagree."

He looked at her eyes. "You're not going to tell Ethan."

"Don't you think he should hear it from us and not someone else?"

He sighed. "Maybe."

"Dad," she said, "what is going on here? I'm just going to come out and say it because obviously you're not going to. Did you do something? To Mom?"

"Jesus. Do you really think that?" he said. "You don't really think that."

"I don't want to think that. Believe me. But you go away and then pull this shit and that night you went ballistic, and I mean, well, all of it, and you're so fucking stupid, Dad, because if you didn't do anything wrong, then you really, really, really need to stop acting like you did."

He stared at her. How did she become this person? When had it happened? Had she always been this wise and bold and thoroughly obnoxious?

"I'm going to go tell Ethan," she said. "And from then on, you can feel free to become the parent here again."

Chapter 14

This beach had been the site of so much bad behavior back in college. Why had they come here? Southie was always in the news then, not that she had paid much attention, but she and Doug had been aware of the lingering unrest after the riots and Whitey Bulger and the bodies that kept turning up. Carson was close to BU, sure, but there were plenty of other places they could have gone. Was it the danger itself that drew them? Danger was a sort of drug when she was in college. They were still infallible, not yet responsible for all that much. She had first tried coke here, huddled around a bonfire with Doug and a handful of other guys. She had skinny-dipped with Doug here, made love in this water, which was filthy then. When she told friends where they had gone and what they had done, the look in their eyes was worth it. "Do you have a death wish?" Sophie asked her once.

Hannah now saw an elderly couple walking their dog on the beach. Two women with white-blond hair stood at the water's edge and watched her lift one foot over the curb and step onto the path that led to the sand. She hugged herself against a bitter breeze. Down a ways, a man sat cross-legged with his chin to his chest. He had his eyes on her too.

Summer was gone. She would probably not step foot on a beach for at least another eight or nine months.

The women walked along the sand. Hannah glanced at her watch. She had to get going. She had to drive the half hour to work; if she left now, she might still be on time.

And if not, well, the girls at the store would easily forgive her. She should have drunk in their respect, their compliments about her new shirt or haircut, her lip gloss. "Can you teach my mom a few things?" Marcy had asked Hannah the other week.

But such words were so often lost on Hannah, and on a bad day they could make her stomach churn, the men in stores who stole glances at her and tentatively asked her the time or where the post office was, the moms at the kids' schools who fawned over Ethan's assist during a soccer game or Janine's viola playing at a school concert or Hannah's handbag or scarf or sunglasses. Hannah was no better, no smarter or kinder than anyone else. She was not unusually interesting or amusing. She was attractive and it got her things that she did not deserve.

Please, Hannah might have said to Marcy or the men or one of those moms. *Please stop.*

Please don't stop. Because without these words, this attention and empty praise, what was there?

Chapter 15

Janine tapped a text into the new cell phone that Lovell had just bought for her to share with Ethan. She had not touched her cereal. Five weeks had passed since Hannah had disappeared. Five weeks and one day.

"I'm going next door after school," Janine said without looking up. "I'm having dinner with the guys."

"Again?" Lovell said. "Is Penelope there?"

"No, although she was there last night. She and Jeff and I played the Princess and the Frog. I was the frog and they were two princesses. It was the cutest thing. She had on this pink-and-purple totally frilly dress that she had brought and they were talking in French and I was *dying*. Stephen took pictures. I kept thinking about how unfair it is that in a lot of places, gay people can't get married and have families. I mean, what the fuck, what kind of messed-up world is this?"

She had spent nearly every evening that week at the neighbors' house, every evening except one, a few days ago, when the five of them had gone out for pizza. Jeff had not stopped complaining about everything from the greasy pizza crust to the loud group of old men behind them to the sweat stains on the cook's T-shirt, which made Janine explode laughing once she saw the shirt for herself. "Ignore Jeff," Stephen told Lovell. "He forgets that he too is *imparfait*." Lovell was more than a little surprised when both Stephen and Jeff let him pick up the bill.

"Why do you have to go there so much?" he asked Janine now. "What if news about Mom comes in?"

"Then walk next door and tell me."

"We miss you here." It might not have sounded genuine, but it was. "Jeff can be a little negative, don't you think?"

Her face changed. "Hey, did I tell you that they are thinking of having a baby?"

"Oh?"

"I might offer to help." She slipped the cell phone into her pocket.

"You mean as a babysitter?"

"Something like that," she said, dropping her eyes as she headed out to her bus stop.

An alarm went off inside Lovell. She could not have meant

what he was now thinking. Could she? No. She had just turned fifteen. He was losing it.

Ethan sat across the table, lost in *The Hobbit,* probably unaware of the absence or presence of any of them. These Tolkien books had been the only ones to hold his attention over the past year. Hannah would have wanted to see this, her son sitting and reading a book, Janine next door with some friends, no matter their age or attitudes. Hannah had worried that Janine focused too much on her studies and her viola. She had so few friends—one or two with whom she discussed homework, but no one else. She never got calls from other girls. She skipped the school dances and class outings. Regardless of how many times Lovell tried to reassure Hannah and remind her that many parents wished their children studied or practiced more, she remained unconvinced.

"Maybe it's her age. Teenagehood is hard," he tried once.

"She's always been uninterested in the other kids." Hannah eyed him, insinuating something.

Well, yes, he too did not have all that many friends, but he had his colleagues. He stayed in loose contact with his college roommate, as well as a couple of other guys from MIT. But Lovell had her, after all, and the kids, and his parents.

SIX WEEKS AFTER Hannah went missing, Detective Duncan called to tell Lovell that an arm bone—a humerus—had been found on Carson. "We can't ID it yet. It's at the lab now. Testing could take a couple months."

Lovell swallowed his breath. "You can't ID it."

"Not yet. Lovell, the case was transferred to Boston Homicide this morning. But it's just a formality. They're better equipped for this sort of thing."

"Oh? Oh."

"The bone? I should probably tell you that it was a woman's. But that's all we know. It could easily be someone else."

It was as if this man kept holding a torch to Lovell's face, retracting it, then pushing it closer.

"Hello?"

"I'm here," Lovell said slowly. "It's really going to take a couple months to get a match?"

"The testing is slow. The labs are backlogged." Duncan went on to explain that the Suffolk County DA's office would assign him a victim witness advocate to give him any more news when it came in and to help him understand it all. "She—or he—will be the next one to call."

More was said over the phone and then nothing and it was time to hang up. The dial tone droned, and then came an abrupt ringing and the brusque schoolmarm's command, "If you'd like to make a call, please hang up and dial again."

Lovell reached up to the counter and set the receiver back in its cradle.

Ethan, his dark hair fluffed at the crown of his head, sat at the table drawing a robot, oblivious. Lovell watched him for a moment. He was a beautiful kid. He would be a handsome man someday. Ethan turned to him. "Dad? Who called?"

"No one," Lovell said. The words came as if from a recording inside him: "It was a friend of your mom's."

"OK." Ethan returned to the table and began to sketch a square on the robot's chest, a door or a control panel.

The din of people and cars and reporters outside the house swelled. The blue lights of a police cruiser flashed against the side of the white refrigerator, on and off, on and off. They had come back. The reporters already knew—hell, they had probably found out before he had.

Chapter 16

Hannah was alone on the beach now except for that man sitting down the way. He got up and began walking toward her. Handsome, he was handsome, and blood sped at the center of her chest.

"You're cold," he said as he approached, and she nodded. She turned toward her car. "You want to wear my sweatshirt?" he called after her. He offered her a dark blue sweatshirt with "University of Massachusetts" silk-screened across the front. It was a strange gesture, a commitment if she had taken him up on it. He looked too old to be in college. He might have been in his mid- to late thirties. Thirty-seven?

"No, thanks," she said. "I should go." Maybe Mrs. Keller would come into the shop today and entertain them with stories of her two sisters who had just gotten jobs at the Franklin

Park Zoo, or maybe one of the girls at the store had gone on a date. Maybe something unexpected would happen.

"I should get going too," he said. "I'm already late for work." He kept his eyes on hers.

"What do you do?" she asked in order to end the silence.

"University," he said, wagging the sweatshirt in his hands, and she understood that he was a graduate student or a professor.

They walked together toward the parking lot. She wondered which car was his—the beat-up Volkswagen, the Chevy? He turned to glance at her face every few seconds, and she became aware that she was being assessed. She was used to this, but now it was not an unpleasant sensation. She half smiled at him.

"Could you give me a ride?" he asked.

"Where?" The train was nearby, she was sure.

He smiled. "UMass?"

"Of course." But she would be too late for work. Then again, she might be late even without this detour. She could tell the girls she hadn't gotten the latest schedule.

He smiled again. *Yes,* she saw him thinking, *yes.* She was pretty.

But he was a stranger and this was Southie, and she said, "Sorry, I can't. I'm late for work too."

"Huh," he said. He lifted his arms and slipped on his sweatshirt. "All right, no worries. I'll take the T."

She thought that UMass had to be only a few T stops away. He watched her hug her purse to her side and drop her eyes.

She must have reeked of uptight suburbia. She had become the sort of person who was actually nervous in a city, the sort that she had once mocked—she had become a sort, period, and it had been so long since she had surprised even herself. "Well, why not? Come on." She went to unlock the passenger door and walked around the back of the car. She got in the driver's seat and he pulled his sweatshirt sleeves down over his fingers to warm himself. "What's your job?" he asked.

"I work in a flower shop."

He said, "You work with dead things? Things that have been cut from their roots and stuck in vases so people can look at them for the last week of their lives."

She laughed. "I've never thought of it that way. What's *your* job?"

"I teach."

"What subject?"

"Guess."

"I don't know," she said. "This way?" she asked, gesturing to the left when she had reached the edge of the lot, and he nodded.

He did not look like any professor that she ever had. Cars idled in a line of traffic perpendicular to them. Someone leaned on a horn, and she rose nearly a foot in her seat. Driving in Boston was the worst. Why had she even come here? She glanced at him and then back at the traffic. He was lean, at least leaner than Lovell, his face more defined and objectively more attractive. What a terrible thought to have. He looked more like a surfer than a professor—maybe he taught something like art. "Art? Or music?"

"Bingo."

"No. Really?"

"Music theory," he said, and she smiled, oddly proud.

"You play an instrument?"

"Sure."

"You're one of these people who plays them all."

He nodded. "Guilty." He curled his sleeve further inside his hand like a mitten and pressed the "on" button on the CD player, and Janine's Beethoven began. He turned the volume nearly all the way up, and the steering wheel pulsed in her hands. "It should be loud. You should be able to feel the notes in your veins."

"Maybe. I guess I'm tired of this CD. It's my daughter's. She plays it constantly."

"How old is she?"

"Fourteen."

"And she's nothing like you."

"Not really. Hey, I can barely hear you," she said, and she turned down the music.

"What *is* your daughter like?"

Hannah did not want to talk about that. "Do you love your job?" she asked him.

He directed her around a small rotary and onto another road. "Sometimes."

"What don't you like about it?"

"Oh, I don't know. The bureaucratic bullshit. The students don't always listen to me. They stare right through me like I'm this inanimate object—a plant or a chair." He tapped his shoe against the dash. "What's your name?" he asked, and she said, "Hannah. And you?"

"James. Jamie."

"You don't look like a James," she said.

"What about Jamie?"

She shrugged, and he said, "What's your husband's name?"

"Lovell," she said. Was this a betrayal? It felt like a small one.

"Do you call him Love?"

"Yes."

"Because you love him or because the word is a part of his name?"

Some membrane between them was missing, one that typically separated her from other people. "That's not your business," she said.

"You're right," he said. "You're pretty, you know."

Her face filled with heat. "Let's get you to work," she said.

He leaned over to eject the CD and found a station playing jazz, some moony song, a single piano and then trumpets and trombones whining, the deep morass of a tuba. Nothing she would typically listen to. Lovell's father adored the stuff. She glanced at the clock and thought that the girls at the shop would have called her at home by now—they did not have her cell phone number. Without traffic, she would be only a half hour late. She would drop him off and then get right on the Pike and call them from her cell, drive directly to work.

"You look like your name," he said.

"In what way?"

"I like it. Hannah, means 'grace,' right? I have a cousin Hannah. She's a nurse for kids with cancer in Seattle. She's something else."

They had reached the campus, and to their right, empty wooden benches overlooked the water. A buoy drifted near the shore and a seagull pecked at it, then lifted into the air. A couple of men in waders were pulling a boat to shore, probably for the winter.

"All right," she said. "I guess this should be good-bye."

Chapter 17

Karen Mekenner called Lovell soon after the arm bone was found to tell him that she and some other moms wanted to plan a vigil for Hannah. "When we heard the news, we thought that someone in town had to do something. I already got permission from a guy I know at Parks and Rec to use the town green. And I'm talking to Pastor McGrew over at Saint Patrick's later this afternoon about saying a few prayers. I mean, I know you guys didn't go there, right?"

"We don't go to church," he said. "I—well, Hannah was raised Catholic."

"Perfect then!" Karen said. "It'd be nice for you to say a few things too, Lovell."

Despite how it may have sounded, the discovery of that arm bone was not in fact news about Hannah. There would be no match for a good long while. How many bodies had turned up in South Boston over the years, men and women both? The detective, Lovell himself, all these people outside the house—no one knew anything at all. This was how he presented the non-news to the kids, and even Janine seemed stunned enough to want to believe him. This was how he defined it to his parents and Hannah's and to her sister.

The thought of Karen's gathering made Lovell want to crawl into his bed and refuse all contact with the world at large, but he knew he had to attend.

ON THE EVENING of the vigil, he and the kids moved toward the front of a group of fifty or so others—Hannah's coworkers and friends in town, a few regular customers from the shop, her dentist, their car mechanic, dozens of people he did not recognize. A small, makeshift platform had been set up with a microphone for those who wanted to say something. It was a bitterly cold November night, and Lovell wished he had thought to wear a scarf and hat. He had agreed to read a Dickinson poem and took the xeroxed copy from his pocket. He did not have the heart to read one of her favorites, those plucky, morbid poems that danced with questions of illness and death. He had been glad to come upon a more hopeful verse, and with a lump in his throat, he read:

Our share of night to bear,
Our share of morning,

Our blank in bliss to fill,
Our blank in scorning.

Here a star, and there a star,
Some lose their way.
Here a mist, and there a mist,
Afterwards—day!

It sounded almost ironic now. When he had read it aloud at home, he had found it poignant but hopeful, and right for the occasion. Somewhat embarrassed, he moved back from the microphone and wrapped his arms around the kids' shoulders. He watched a line of women sing "Amazing Grace." Karen Mekenner stood next to the head of the PTO at Ethan's school. As they sang, the women cupped their hands around white taper candles that they held, trying to shield the flames. Here they stood, these pleasant, "athletic stay-at-home moms" who had scraped against Hannah's sense of herself, who had not mirrored what she had wanted them to; here they stood, their faces on the ground, already grieving her, this woman whom they hardly knew. They were innocuous and lovely, nearly heartbreaking in all their naïveté and kindness.

Sophie and her husband appeared at the back of the group with their eyes trained on the ground. She wore a long trench coat and, from what he could see, a colorful silk scarf. Her short black hair had grown out somewhat. She was petite and stood only to her husband's shoulders. Lovell imagined her watching him up front on the platform, the kids on either side of him. From where she stood, it would appear that he was the one leading the vigil tonight.

A priest stepped forward and began to recite a prayer. Everyone bowed their heads as they took in his words. Hannah's attachment to Catholicism had grown tenuous, but it remained fundamental to her. They had married, against his initial wishes, at Saint Margaret on Martha's Vineyard, where she had gotten confirmed so many years ago. "I like the sense that someone else is responsible for us as a couple—that we're not totally alone in this thing that so many people have failed at."

"But remember, you're marrying a nonbeliever."

She replied, "We're not going to Vegas or some random justice of the peace."

"I didn't say we should do that."

"You got to decide about the proposal. You up and asked me right there on my parents' boat. We'd never even talked about it."

"What an awful thing to do, propose."

She only rolled her eyes. "I just want to have a say. I want to make some of the decisions."

"Do you even—" he began. "Do you want to marry me?"

"I don't want to *not* marry you," she said. "Hey—I don't want you to walk away from me. I don't want to leave." She shook her head. "My parents have already booked the church. Forget I said anything. I want to get married. I do."

He had thought that he would never meet anyone else like her. He loved her. He wanted her to be his wife, and he wanted to no longer worry about whether she would leave him.

JANINE CONTINUED TO spend afternoons next door with the neighbors, when she did not have viola lessons or orchestra practice. She began to adopt what he assumed were Stephen's mannerisms and sayings. She complained about her "butch but hetty" art teacher. She complained about Lovell's cooking, his clothing, the fact that he needed "mad grooming." Her comment about Jeff and Stephen's wanting to have a baby began to gnaw at him again.

He made himself just come out and ask her one evening: "How is it that you plan to help Stephen and Jeff with their baby?"

She reached for a pear in the bowl on the kitchen table. "You are shitting yourself right now, aren't you?"

"Well?"

"It's my body. I get to make my own choices."

His own body went cold. "You already proved that when you cut off all your hair. Listen, you just turned fifteen. You are a kid. And you live in my house and I am the adult here."

She licked her front teeth. "It's just sad that not everyone in our country gets to make their own choices."

"Have you talked to them about it yet?"

"No."

"Are you going to?"

"Maybe. Probably."

"When?"

"When I feel like it."

"Will you at least think seriously about it?" Lovell said.

"I am doing that. I'm not an idiot."

"Well, frankly, this would be an idiotic decision."

"Just because they're gay doesn't mean they shouldn't be able to have kids."

He felt himself grow warm. "Can't they adopt? Why the hell is this your responsibility?"

"Because they're my friends. They're more than friends—I love them."

"You love them?" He rolled his eyes. "You love them. Come on."

"Yes, I love them, and they really want a baby. And no, they don't want to adopt. They want the baby to have at least some of their genes."

Maybe this was a fantasy for her, one that they would hopefully never entertain. She'd had plenty of fantasies before. After 9/11, she had threatened to run away because he and Hannah refused to drive her down to New York to help search through the World Trade Center wreckage for bodies. A year earlier, she had begged him and Hannah to let a new kid at her school move into their house, a kid who lived with his family at a homeless shelter in the next town. She was always trying to fight some cause or injustice in some completely absurd, if touching, way.

He said, "Jeff and Stephen also might not want the baby to have a teenage mother who lives next door. Would you—" he began. "Would you mind if I had a talk with them?"

"Shit. Yes, I would. You barely even know them. I don't want my *daddy* marching over there."

He sighed. He looked over at her.

"Don't even think about going over there without telling me, bitch," she said.

"You did not just call me that. I'm not your bitch."

"Oh, please," she groaned.

"I am not gay—and I don't think you are either, you know." He couldn't help himself.

Chapter 18

If you wouldn't mind, the building is just around that bend." Jamie gestured toward an adjacent parking lot.

"Now where?" Hannah asked. She waited for his reply. "Hey, I'm already going to be late for work."

She finally pulled into a spot facing the harbor and shifted into park. "You're going to be late too," she said. "Right?"

He leaned his head back against the seat and inhaled through his nose. "It's Mingus," he said. "Young Duke. He asked his shrink to write the liner notes for this record." The song ended and another came on, a discordant piece that made Hannah edgy as she always was with this sort of music, the unpredictable beat, those sudden stops and starts. He went on: "My folks sent me to a shrink a couple times when I was a kid, but the man was kind of boring. I felt bad for him, really."

She half turned toward him.

"I'm sorry. Why would you care about that? I guess I must not want to work today. I must be trying to stall, going on and on as if someone like you would have any interest."

"Someone like me?"

"You don't exactly project instability."

"Really? I've been in therapy. The last time was a few years ago, once my kids were old enough and I had the time," she said. "It didn't take. The doctor was a lot younger. I think she found *me* boring."

"No," he said.

"Yeah, well, I wasn't abused or anything. I wasn't anorexic or bulimic or schizophrenic."

"What were you?"

She thought a moment. "Me."

"That woman wasn't bored. She was jealous," he said. He turned to her. His eyes moved from one side of her face to the other. "Why do you sell flowers?"

No one had ever asked her this, not even Lovell. "I don't know. I've done it since college. I used to deliver them."

"Because it made people happy when they opened their doors and saw *you* holding all those flowers?"

"Could be."

His fingers fiddled beneath his sleeves, and his feet tapped as if an explosive were hidden just beneath his surface. "Do you like me?"

"I don't know—I don't know you." Her hands grew cold

against the steering wheel. She gradually lowered them along the smooth circle until they rested at either end of its diameter.

"People know these things within seconds. They know who they like and who they don't and who they trust." At last he looked away. "I like you."

"Well, I guess I don't *dislike* you," she said.

"I'm making you uncomfortable."

She half shrugged. She did not want to agree with him, nor did she want to disagree.

"I still have a few more minutes before class starts. Let's take a quick walk down by the water. You can't beat the view here." He unlatched his seat belt. "You want to call your work and tell them you'll be a few minutes late?"

"I guess I should," she said. She reached for her cell phone in the glove compartment.

"Hannah!" Marcy said. "We were wondering where you were." Her young, high voice was a surprise. Hannah's life was a world away.

"Janine is home sick," Hannah said. She heard Mozart in the background, *Eine kleine Nachtmusik,* played on loop there from morning to closing time. "But I'll come in soon, in about half an hour or so. She'll just stay home and sleep today. Sorry about this."

"It's OK," Marcy said.

Jamie looked at Hannah as she apologized again before saying good-bye.

"Why didn't you tell her the truth?" he asked.

"What am I supposed to do, tell her I'm sitting in my car in Boston with some guy I just met?"

"I never lie," he said with surprising earnestness. "Ask me anything."

"Do you really work here?" She only realized that this had been a question for her after the words had left her mouth.

"I really do. Professor Trobec or Professor T., they call me. Today's lecture is 'Conflicting Ideologies in the Analysis of Jazz,'" he said.

She paused and said, "Sounds conflicting in another way, jazz and ideology."

"Yes. Hence the conflict." He stepped out of the car and walked around the back to open her door for her. "Come on now, Hannah, let's go for that walk." He offered his left hand, and she took it for a second, then let it go.

They made their way over a hillside that sloped toward a sidewalk and then the water. They passed a few college kids smoking, one a girl in black army pants and a yellow T-shirt, and then a young father with a baby in a stroller. Hannah thought of Janine and Ethan and his big green backpack tight around his shoulders that morning. She would leave soon. This strange moment and this person, this man, would become a memory. "I don't come into the city too often," she admitted, as if to explain something about her behavior.

"Why not?"

"Well, the kids, and my job. Our lives aren't here."

"*Our lives?* What do you and your husband like to do?"

"The usual stuff, I guess."

"Oh, that."

"Are you married?" she asked.

"Don't believe in it."

"Why not? You're the noncommittal type?"

"I'm committed to not marrying," he said. Speaking to him was a little like looking into a fun-house mirror.

She took in the panorama before her, the marbled sky and the opaque water, the buoys along the horizon. She tried to remember what this water and sky had looked like so many years ago with Doug, the moment before he suggested they get married and the moment after.

"I'll admit that I can't stand the thought of walking into that big gray lecture hall and seeing all those bored faces."

She nodded. "I can imagine."

"Because how often do I get to see a face like yours?" He suddenly shook his head back and forth like a wet dog. "Wait. What day is it?"

"Thursday."

"Ha! What do you know?" he said. "This whole time I've been thinking today was Wednesday. Lucky you. I don't have that class today after all."

Chapter 19

Not long after the vigil, Janine told Lovell that the neighbors were planning a costume party for the next night. "They wanted me to invite you and Ethan. So I guess you're invited."

"Oh? Sounds fun," Lovell said.

"You don't have to come."

"You don't want us there," he said, but he thought that the party might be a chance to get a better handle on her fixation with these guys, maybe even a clearer sense of the rationale behind this asinine surrogacy business. It would also be a good alternative to sitting at home, thinking and worrying about Hannah. "But I think we should go," he said.

Janine would wear one of Lovell's old button-down shirts and his dark blue bathrobe; she would be Beethoven. The next day, Lovell helped Ethan assemble a pirate costume, Captain Jack Sparrow, he insisted—pants that he had outgrown and that now looked more like knickers, along with one of Janine's shirts, a white summer blouse with capped sleeves and a cinched waist. "It's so girly," Ethan protested, but Lovell told him that pirates did in fact wear girly shirts. Lovell typically wore vampire fangs and a red cape when he passed out candy each Halloween, despite Hannah's attempts to stoke his middling enthusiasm for the holiday. "We could be some kind of duo. Robert Browning and Elizabeth Barrett? The Alcotts?" she suggested once. He had just gone for his plastic fangs in response. With no other easy options now, he went to find them again.

Stephen and Jeff welcomed the three of them at the door that night. Stephen wore a long black wig threaded with gold braids. He was Cleopatra, and Jeff was Mark Antony, draped in a white sheet, a ring of plastic ivy on his head. Lovell tried to turn off his growing distaste for these men—they could very well become his allies.

Lovell stood by the bar, a card table set up in the corner of the room, while Janine chatted with a man dressed as Princess Di. The living room had been transformed into a gothic nightclub. The walls had been covered in mirrored wrapping paper splattered with black paint. Lovell wondered what this place typically looked like; it was tough to imagine, given the scene right now. In each corner stood tall green statues of gargoyles wearing plastic Groucho Marx glasses. The lamps had been turned off, and a lone purple bulb dangled from the ceiling and lent everyone a shaded, haunted look. A thumping, rhythmic song played, possibly an Indian singer and sitar that had been grafted onto a hip-hop beat. In the center of the room, a small cluster of men danced and mouthed the words of the song.

Ethan set up camp on the couch behind a ceramic lettuce leaf filled with olives, his eyes on two men now lip-locked on the dance floor. Was this whole scene a little much for him? Lovell took a seat next to him and watched Janine pass by, balancing a bowl of chips in one hand and a goblet that sloshed with pink liquid in the other. What exactly was in the glass?

Lovell was about to say something to her when Stephen appeared beside a gargoyle and Janine pranced over to him and perched on the arm of an easy chair. Here they were, Beethoven and Cleopatra, old friends. Potential surrogate and donor? Of course getting pregnant would be the ultimate middle finger to this "messed up" world.

Stephen and Jeff had moved here just before Hannah disappeared. Lovell remembered approaching them on the sidewalk one evening as they were unloading a U-Haul. He introduced himself and offered opinions about where to find good pizza and a decent dry cleaner nearby. Stephen went to move their Prius into the driveway, and Lovell said to Jeff, "Can we start a club for people here who don't drive minivans or underpay Brazilians to overwater their lawns?"

Jeff appeared horrified. "Our guy, Victor, owns his own business."

Lovell fumbled for an apology.

The smell of incense, sandalwood maybe or sage, hit him. Bodies moved in a hot swarm. Someone's sweaty arm brushed his hand, the purple bulb flickered above, the nasal sitar twanged the same note again and again. Lovell took it all in. He tried to imagine Hannah there with him, gazing out at this dark room that might as well have been miles and miles from their home, but he could not seem to place her here. He ran through how things might have been different if she had not gone away. Janine might not have befriended Stephen and Jeff. She might not have shaved her head; she might not be wishing that she were carrying their baby right now. And if he and Hannah had not had their fight, if she had only paid that one bill? The variables began to multiply in his mind.

He wondered whether Hannah had considered leaving him during times other than the one night she spent at her sister's. Her sarcastic suggestions about his choice of words or shoes later evolved into orders not to slouch, not to play so many computer games, orders that eventually, soon after they got engaged, melted into judgments. Whenever he was home, he was so rarely "present." He promised to try harder, and he did for a while. He made sure to comment on a new recipe and laugh each and every time she told a joke. But after a while, the focus of her irritation broadened. He spoke "too quietly," "too loudly," "too quickly," "too much about work." He seldom, if ever, exhibited any interest in her daily life. He never asked her any questions about anything anymore. And the kids too—why didn't he ever ask them about their days or school or friends? He drifted around their house, burrowed deep in his thoughts a good 90 percent of the time, and what would this do to them, other than show Ethan that it was acceptable for men not to interact with those around them, and Janine that she was unworthy of his attention?

Lovell said something like, "I am doing the best that I can. Forgive me if I'm not perfect one hundred percent of my life," and she replied, "That is a cop-out if I've ever heard one." Over time, her unending complaints became like sandpaper that scratched raw a big part of him. Each new round made him sting and wriggle away. "You will never be happy with anything," he shot back. "You're not happy with yourself, and no one else is good enough for you." Each new round eroded her aura of sweet mystery and the welcome surprise of her bluntness and even her beauty itself. She was right in front of him then, right up in his face, so close that he could no longer see her.

"Where did your sister go?" he asked Ethan. Lovell could not see Janine anywhere. Ethan shrugged.

Lovell elbowed his way across the dance floor and toward the kitchen, where a few men sat around a table covered in bottles of vodka and gin. "Anyone seen Beethoven?" he asked them. They just looked at him. He might as well have been dressed up as Anxious Straight Man.

He headed toward a staircase and followed voices until he reached a bedroom. He stopped before pushing open the door and tried to hear what he could: Janine's voice, and maybe Stephen's as well. He pressed his ear to the door just as the door flew open and Janine stumbled on top of him.

"Were you listening in on us?" she asked.

"Home. We're going home." He reached for her elbow and led her toward the stairs, although she twisted in his grip.

"I'm not ready to go yet. I want to stay," she said, but he pushed her forward.

Outside, Janine collided with Ethan and tripped down the stoop, landing on her side across the brick walk. Thankfully, the news vans had left—those that had shown up after the discovery of that arm bone a few days ago. Lovell held tight to her hand across the lawn and the shallow gulley that separated the properties, up onto their own lawn, and toward the house. Ethan followed behind them. "What were you guys talking about?" Lovell finally asked.

"Nothing. Fuck."

"Why were you hiding in a bedroom?"

"That is in no way your business," Janine said.

Once inside, Lovell pulled the front door closed behind him, and both kids disappeared upstairs.

Minutes later, he heard a slam and the sound of Janine throwing up. "Janine?" he called, beginning up the stairs. She appeared at the top, her mouth wet and her eyes swollen, her wig in her hand like a small carcass. "I need my bed," she groaned.

He turned to Ethan, who was watching from his doorway,

and tried to keep a measured tone. "Give us a sec. She'll be all right."

Lovell followed Janine as she slumped into her bedroom and began to shed her costume. She stood beside her metal music stand, shivering and coughing in a white cotton bra and purple striped underwear. She was narrower through the shoulders than he had remembered. He had not seen her without clothes on in so long. Her shaved head was pinkish and looked exposed. His frustration evaporated; he had the urge to scoop her up and set her in a deep, warm nest. "Sit," he said.

"I think I just puked all the drunk out of me. My brain feels like a fucking bowling ball." She fell back across her mattress.

Lovell looked in vain through her dresser to find pajamas. At last he found a green flannel nightgown on the floor in the corner of the room.

She sat back up and covered her face with her hands. When she took them away, she turned her bloodshot eyes to Lovell and scanned his face and his hair and his arms as he shook the nightgown straight. "You two always fought. You couldn't stand each other."

"Janine." He stopped.

"The night before—that was one of your worst. It *was* your worst."

He set the nightgown next to her on the bed.

She reached for it and eased herself back up into a standing position. She lifted the nightgown over her head and slid her arms inside. She looked at him, measuring his reaction. "I kept the evidence, you know." Janine rummaged around in one of her drawers and produced a plastic bag with shards of broken and shattered glass inside.

"What is that?"

"It used to be her perfume. You don't remember decimating it? Are you kidding me?"

He blinked at her. "It fell off the counter."

"You were so off the hook. You think I couldn't hear every-thing? Go into your bathroom and I'll make noise. You tell me what you can hear. I thought you might actually knock down the wall."

He shook his head. She was being dramatic, as always.

"And you almost hit her. I saw it. I saw you going toward her."

"Jesus. Listen to you. You need to stop this. Yes, we had a fight. Yes, we said some not-so-nice things. And yes, her per-fume fell. But there's no need to exaggerate here and pretend you heard things—and saw things—that you know perfectly well you didn't." He had been hard enough on himself. He did not need her help in heaping on the blame. "You've had a lot to drink tonight, and by the way, alcohol is illegal at your age."

"Is it? I wasn't aware of that." Her words were slurred. She fingered the white collar of her nightgown. "I saw Mom in the bedroom, you know, while you were locked in the bathroom. I went in and checked on her. She was sitting alone on your bed and crying. She was probably terrified. I sure as shit was. Anyway, she was such a mess that she didn't even notice I was there. And I saw you about to deck her. I did. And then you slammed the door so I couldn't see any more. I can't believe you're acting like I'm lying. It all doesn't look so good right now, does it?"

"Janine, I want you to think very carefully about what you are saying."

Her eyes fell to the ground.

"It was unfortunate, of course it was, but it wasn't as bad as you're saying. Adults fight sometimes. You know that," Lovell tried. "Why didn't you ever tell me all of this?"

"Maybe I was scared."

"Of what?"

"Duh. Of what you might do to me?"

"Are you serious? Did I ever even spank you? Have I ever even come close?" He glanced down at the bag of crushed glass. "Did you show that to anyone—the police?"

Janine shook her head.

He reached toward her, but she batted away his hand. "I didn't want you to get in trouble," she finally said. "Because what the hell would happen to us then?" Her eyes began to fill. "You can be a total dick. But you are still my father." She finally set the plastic bag on her dresser. She cried quietly for a while, and it was unbearable not to be able to touch her or comfort her right now.

She lay on her bed again, this time on her side, her arms around her knees. "Maybe she wouldn't have gone off if you hadn't been such a complete and total shithead to her that night."

He blinked at her. He could not disagree. He had no argument at all. "I'm sorry we had that fight. Every day I'm sorry. I've never been more sorry about anything," he finally said.

"What do you think happened to her?"

"I genuinely don't know, sweetheart."

"Do you think she'll be OK?"

"I do," he said automatically. "I really do. I really hope she'll come back. I think she will. We have to think that, right?" Lovell steadied himself against the wall. "It's been a long night. Everything seems worse at night, believe me, especially after too many drinks. Try to get some sleep." He turned out the light. Just before he closed the door, he said, "Why did you keep the glass all this time?"

"To give back to Mom."

"But it was—"

"I know. I thought there might still be a little perfume left on the pieces. I wasn't really thinking. I couldn't sleep later that night, so I went into your bathroom and all the glass was still there and so I gathered it up. I think you were downstairs or something. I figured I'd give it to her the next morning, but I didn't really get the chance, and then I thought I could give it to her that afternoon."

"I don't think I slept at all that night." The daylight, he remembered, was a sort of medicine. Truly nothing was as acute or upsetting in the first light of day.

She looked at him. "Is that—was what you did that night like domestic violence?"

"Janine, I didn't touch her. No matter how angry I was, I would not have hurt her. Or you. I'd never hurt any of you. That's not who I am. I can't believe I even have to tell you these things."

"Well, you sure as hell touched her perfume and our walls. It sure as shit sounded violent to me. You sure said some nasty things to her."

"You've made your point," he finally said. He could stand here all night, getting nowhere. "Now get some sleep." He shut off the light and pulled the door closed behind him.

The only light nearby was a small, moon-shaped night-light outside Ethan's closed door that emitted a dim yellow glow. Somewhere a clock ticked. He tried to gather himself as he considered all that had just happened. Janine had held these things inside for two months now. He had never known her to keep anything inside. She had been that afraid of him—or that afraid that he would be carted away by the police.

It was inconceivable that they were all in the center of this hell right now and that he himself had brought them all to this dark, airless place.

He crept toward Ethan's bedroom and carefully pushed open his door. Ethan lay asleep on top of his quilt, still in his costume, his eye patch against his cheek now. Lovell moved his koala next to his head and slipped out of his bedroom.

Lovell headed toward his bedroom, nudged forward the half-open door, and stood at the end of the king-size bed, looking over at the gold-and-turquoise damask comforter, the matching pillows set side by side, the identical wooden end tables with identical antique lamps, their nut-brown shades hung with amber beads, an ivory wool shag carpet at the foot of the bed.

The bed was positioned directly beneath a large skylight, now a saturated black. Lovell realized that he would never get any sleep in this room. He gathered the comforter and a pillow and lugged them down the hallway and onto the stairs. He spread out the comforter across the long couch in the living room. He looked over at the many shadows on the walls, the silhouettes of branches bobbing in the wind.

Chapter 20

They were not alone, at least. Thousands of students moved in and around the buildings behind them. Hannah turned from Jamie and walked briskly toward the lot, concerned that he might try to catch up with her, but when she looked back, he stood frozen, his eyes on her. She moved her gaze to the huddle of brick buildings before her. She would not give him the satisfaction of turning around again. But as she tripped over the curb and onto the concrete, she became aware of herself half rushing, half walking in a frenzied escape toward her car, a nervous woman thrown into a tizzy by a friendly stranger. And she could not help glancing back again, and there he stood in that same spot. He lifted his hand in a happy wave. She had overreacted to harmless flirtation. She had overestimated her own impact on him.

When she reached her car, she saw from the corner of her eye Jamie walking near the water. It was hard to know in which direction he was headed. She waited before she opened her door. She would take just another moment to show him that she was more than she had appeared. She leaned her head back and tried to look as though she were enjoying one last breath of ocean air. When she lowered her face again, there he was, walking toward her. He cocked his head as he came closer, stepping through the space between them, and she instinctively pushed her hand against his chest and felt the thumping beneath his shirt. She pulled back—she had kept her hand there for too long. But he did not move away. He just squinted, evaluating her eyes, and then he kissed her.

"Jesus," she said as she pulled away, dizzy and short of breath. It seemed as if she had just woken after the longest sleep to find herself inside a burning room. *I am Hannah Hall*, she thought. *I have children and a husband.* She looked down at his watch and saw that it was already past noon. She could—now and always—feel nothing more acutely than time and with it the urgency of the next task. She had gotten this from her mother, she felt sure, this innate discipline. "Goodbye again," Hannah said, and she reached for the door handle.

Chapter 21

Ten weeks after Hannah had disappeared, one month after Lovell learned about the arm bone, another detective from Homicide in Boston called him at work to say that a section of a metatarsal, or a bone from a foot—a woman's—had been found behind a Burger King in Roxbury.

"God," Lovell said.

"I wanted you to hear it from me and not those reporters outside your house."

Was Lovell expected to thank him? Lovell's mind raced: *Hannah is Hannah, not some bones somewhere. This is not her, this is not Tu.* "You can't ID it though."

"Not at this point."

He wanted to say, *Come back to me when you have*

something definitive, because this slow dribble of non-news? These updates that are not in fact updates? These are bullshit.

His colleague Lucinda stood watching him just outside his office. They had worked together for a decade.

"Lovell," she said after he hung up, her face contorted with sympathy. She stepped into his office. She had coarse gray hair to her waist and wore a plaid dress with a white cardigan. She already knew, of course. She had probably read about it online. It was unbearable, the speed with which everyone else learned the news that he had only just learned himself.

"Luce."

"You shouldn't be here."

"Where else should I be?"

She just shook her head. She was only a few years older than him, but she could have been his aunt or even his grandmother.

"They can't ID it. They don't know anything at this point."

"Go home and sit by the phone. You should be there for your kids."

"I'm always there for them."

She nodded sadly.

"The numbers from NOAA just came in."

"So?" She left his office and returned a moment later with a cardboard banker's box. "Get what you need and bring it home. I'll tell everyone here. You can call in for staff meetings if we need you." She stood there, waiting for him to pack up his office. She was not going anywhere. "Don't come back here until it makes sense."

"All right," he finally said.

"And Lovell? The kids."

"I'm doing the best I can, Luce. Cut me some slack, all right? I can't be with them twenty-four-seven."

"I was going to say you ought to call their schools and get them excused."

"Oh."

"When you're done packing up, you close your door here and you do that. OK? Tell the schools that you don't know when they're going to come back." She began to button up her cardigan. When she was finished, she crossed her arms. "You'll do that?"

THAT EVENING, LUCINDA e-mailed Lovell the name of a psychologist who worked primarily with kids who had lost parents or siblings. "Feel free to ignore this if you want—I don't mean to intrude. But she is supposed to be really good," Lucinda wrote.

He wanted to remind her that his kids had not officially lost anyone. That no one was mourning anyone just yet. He began to type a response, but the sight of his words on the screen—the hard tone of them—made him stop. Ethan had begun sleepwalking again. For all Lovell knew, his daughter was pregnant. When he had told them about the foot bone that afternoon, he had reminded them that no match had been made and that murders were unfortunately not unheard of in Boston, so this really could have come from anyone. They listened and blinked and believed him, he thought. Even Janine, who said, "Grown-ups can be horrible people." These moments would probably color the rest of their lives. "What's her number?" he finally wrote to Lucinda.

Janine was reluctant when Lovell presented the idea. "I don't know. I mean, I assumed that you'd want us to talk to *someone*," she said. "Is it a man or a woman?"

"Woman."

"Figures."

"What?"

"That you wouldn't want us talking to a man," she said.

"What does that mean? Would you rather see a man?"

"It makes no difference to me, Dad."

"I have no idea what to say to you anymore."

"That's because you are really limited when it comes to emotions."

"I am your father. If it weren't for me, you wouldn't be here," he said. He added, "It'd be good if you were a little nicer to me."

"Maybe you need to earn it."

He burned with the urge to slap her. "This," he said, using whatever restraint he could muster, "can be something you talk about with the therapist." He walked out of the room and called upstairs for Ethan.

"What is this doctor gonna want to know?" Ethan asked.

"Probably whatever you want to tell her," Lovell answered. "She's there to help you get through this stuff."

"Well, who is she?" Ethan asked.

"Listen, Lucinda said this woman is supposed to be really smart. Although you may not believe this, I do worry about you guys. A lot."

"That must be why you pawn us off on Grandma all the time," Janine said. Lovell could not have traveled to Los Angeles without his mother's help. Since his return, he had been relying on her to drive them to some practices and other activities.

"Would you rather I had pulled you out of all your after-school stuff because there was no way I could get home in time to pick you up?"

Both kids glared at him. He instantly felt guilty.

"Fine, I'll go. But I'm only saying what *I* want to say," Janine insisted. "She can't make me act like some big victim."

"Believe me, no one thinks of you that way," Lovell said. Janine and Ethan began to walk away, and Lovell said, "Also, I think you guys should take a break from school for a while."

"Why?" Ethan asked.

Lovell should have thought this through. He looked at his kids, side by side in front of him. "There's just too much going on right now."

"But you said that bone was someone else's," Ethan said.

"I did, I know." Lovell's heart dropped. "I just think it's a good idea." Why had he told Lucinda that he would do this? Maybe it would be better for them to continue on with their daily routines.

"OK," Janine said somberly.

"You can do your schoolwork at home. I'll call your teachers and ask them to send us a bunch of stuff. And we can go see this doctor and be together, and I promise, it'll all work out."

DR. VALMER'S OFFICE was two towns away, in the attic of her stately Tudor home, a dusty but happy-looking space with heavy yellow and gold tapestries draped from the slanted eaves and a patchwork of amber and brown Turkish carpets on the scuffed wood floor. Dr. Valmer had suggested she meet with the two kids together. "If they want to come to me on their own sometimes, that's fine too," she had said over the phone. She had sounded as if she recognized Lovell's name, maybe from the news, but she had not admitted as much.

Lovell walked Janine and Ethan toward a white couch and hovered behind them. Dr. Valmer was a middle-aged Germanic-looking woman with spiky blond hair and a red silk scarf patterned with fruit. Lovell waited for her to say something, maybe pull him aside for a chat before they started. Janine lifted off a knit skullcap to reveal her short hair. Ethan began to chew on a thumbnail. "OK," Lovell said. "So, anything else?"

"We're ready to start," Dr. Valmer said.

"I guess I'll come back in fifty minutes?"

She nodded, and the floor creaked beneath him as he made his way out of the room and back down the stairs. He got into his car and sat for a moment, wondering whether he had done the right thing by bringing them here. The conversation he'd had with the doctor over the phone had been cursory, a couple of questions from her about how long Hannah had been gone, the names and ages of the kids. What if there was some sort of grief counseling being pushed on them right now? Talk of death and healing and moving on, all of that? He should have told the doctor more, the state of the case and all the questions that remained.

This was a neighborhood of towering Victorians and Tudors, slate walkways, three-car garages, and sprawling, mature trees. In Dr. Valmer's driveway a silver Mercedes sat before a copper-roofed pergola that, from what he could see, led to an enormous, sloped backyard, now coated in snow. How much would this woman up in that office really comprehend about their lives? And his troubles with Hannah, her disappearance, the dribble of shadowy updates, this dark, unpredictable new world in which he and the kids lived—what could Dr. Valmer or anyone else really do to fix any of that?

He stayed in his car for the remainder of their session, listening to news radio. He could not think of what else to do.

"They did nicely," she said when he went back inside the house to pick them up. She suggested the two come twice weekly. "You and I should set up a time to touch base in a week or so."

"Sure, yeah," he said, and he went for his checkbook.

Janine had already slid on her jacket and skullcap and moved toward the door.

"So?" he said once they were in the car.

"Can you turn on the radio?" Ethan asked.

Lovell shifted into drive. "Tell me how it went first."

"It went," Janine said.

"Did you like her?"

"She talked a lot," Ethan said. "Radio?"

"What did she say? What did you guys talk about?"

"The Red Sox. The weather," Janine joked. "And Mom, of course. And you."

Lovell drove through the neighborhood and came to a stop sign, skidding briefly on a patch of ice. "Did it seem like she knew what she was doing?"

Janine, her eyes still out the window, said, "As much as anyone does."

"She gave us peppermints," Ethan added.

"Oh?" Lovell said hopefully.

"They were gross," Janine said.

"But do you think she was helpful?" Lovell tried again.

"She's a little *traditional*," Janine said.

"Meaning?"

"Like, she was asking about how it was for us not to have someone to do our laundry and cook for us these days."

"Well, that's a piece of this," he said.

Janine looked at him in the rearview mirror.

"No?"

"Mom's more than just our maid."

"Of course she is—was. Is." Not one part of this was easy.

He wanted to know more about what approach Dr. Valmer had taken. Had they opened up to her right away? Or had she just taken this session to get to know them? Did she have a plan for them? He wondered what they had told her, whether they had even begun to talk about Hannah's disappearance. Or maybe they just talked about Hannah herself? And him—what exactly had they told the doctor about him?

WHEN THE TIME came for Lovell to meet with her, Dr. Valmer greeted him in the cramped waiting area that had been set up outside her office, her red reading glasses halfway down her nose. "Hi there." She smiled and ushered him forward. A heart-shaped bowl of individually wrapped peppermints sat on the coffee table before the white couch. "I've heard about these mints," he said as he moved before the couch. "But not much else."

She sat opposite him on a rust-colored wingback chair, her worn black flats propped on a crocheted stool cushion. "They're great kids," she began.

"I think so."

"Janine's exploring some different identities."

"You mean her hair? Yeah, that was a surprise. I wasn't totally in favor of it. I only found out after the fact."

"And the gay neighbors."

"She's not gay. She just wants to get knocked up and carry their child," he tried to joke.

Dr. Valmer looked at him. "She's exerting control during

a time when there is little of this. She's angry. She's grieving. They both are. They miss their mom. Sounds like she was an incredible woman."

He crossed his arms over his chest. "We may not have reached the point of grief yet."

"Meaning?"

"We don't have all the information here. There's still a lot of evidence that's not come in."

She nodded slowly, as if diagnosing him with something. She tilted her head. "So tell me about your wife."

"Hannah was pretty great."

"Have you talked to anyone about everything that's happened? Any counselors?"

"Not yet. I probably should."

"If you decide you'd like some names, let me know." She gazed at him kindly.

"I guess you're primarily here for the kids."

"I am," she said. "But there are plenty of names of good people I could give you." She rose with a flourish, went to the corner of the room, and shuffled through some papers behind her desk. "So, Janine and Ethan and I are creating what I like to call a 'lasting legacy' for their mother. Here it is." She produced a wide black scrapbook with the word *Memories* inscribed in gold on the front.

Lovell went cold. He thought about telling her, *Thank you, but we're all done here. You won't be seeing my kids again.*

"Go ahead, you can look," she said.

"This isn't confidential?" he tried.

"They know you're going to see it. They're making it for the three of you as a family."

She waited for him. He had no choice but to lift the front cover. On the first page he saw a rectangular white label with the words "Our Mother." Under it, in various colors of Magic Marker, they had written: *Thoughtful. Nice. Loved flowers. Pretty. Good mom. Great cook. Liked holidays.* Lovell adjusted his posture and turned to the next page, where beneath another label marked "Important Moments" he saw small objects that had been attached with Scotch tape: an old elephant-shaped birthday card for Ethan, a postcard sent to Janine her first year at sleepaway camp.

Lovell shrank into his seat.

"What is it like for you to see this?" she asked.

He looked up at her. "A little weird, I guess," he managed. He had the sense that his family and their messy, wonderful, excruciating lives had been placed inside some hulking steel machine, flattened into a piece of paper, cut into the shape of a heart, and run through a laminator. "I didn't know that—I mean, I guess I thought you'd be talking with them about other things."

"Yes?"

"I just wonder, you know, will this actually help them? Is it really making them feel better?" He had imagined more talking and crying, less arts and crafts. More talk of fear and anxiety, less talk of remembrance.

She peered at him from above her reading glasses.

"I mean, it's really nice that they're doing this," he said.

"I'm trying to help them turn a negative memory fraught with trauma into a more positive one."

"Good luck with that," he said.

"They need to reclaim their power of agency, Lovell. Victims of violence find these kinds of activities incredibly helpful."

"Did Janine let you use that word, 'victim'?"

"I didn't need to."

He turned the page and saw a list that the kids had made under the heading, "Favorite Things": *Emily Dickinson, the Red Sox, classical music, kiwi fruit, the ocean.* "If you think it's working."

"You seem to think it's important that this process *work* for them. You've used that word more than once."

"I guess I do."

"It's a process. The setting down of memories. You might remember this too. The process matters. The journey itself." She looked at him. "And just so you know, Janine really does want to carry the neighbors' child. She's also thinking about getting her tongue pierced. I suggested she talk it over with you first."

"Holy hell."

"And Ethan sometimes sleepwalks. He's been going into Janine's room, but she helps him back to bed. And he's worried and more than a little embarrassed about his stutter. You might call up his old speech therapist?"

"I know that. I live with the kid. I already have a call in to her," he lied. Ethan sleepwalked to Janine's room now?

"Good. So I'll see them again tomorrow?" she said.

He nodded but told himself to give these appointments some more thought.

Chapter 22

Once inside her car, Hannah jammed her key into the ignition, started the engine, and shifted into reverse. She pulled out of the spot and forward, but a pickup cut in front of her. She glared at its gray bumper as she slowed toward the exit. "Move, come on," she said aloud. The driver rode the brakes, waving at other cars to go ahead. Jamie stood again motionless in her rearview mirror, gradually growing smaller, his arms crossed. Unsurprised.

She watched the bumper before her, her foot pulsing on the brake, as she inched toward the exit. She tried to think of what to tell Marcy and Jen. *Janine was worse off than I thought. It was a stomach bug and the poor thing could hardly stand up and*—it would be easy. And even if Hannah did not say a thing, even if she blazed into the store without any explanation of her further delay, Jen, the manager, would hardly confront her. Jen was twenty-four and painfully introverted, a gap-toothed, freckled girl whose father owned the shop and one other in Wayland. Hannah could vaguely apologize to them, and Jen would avert her eyes and say, *Don't worry. It's been quiet here.* For the rest of Hannah's shift, the shop would remain empty—there rarely were any customers in the middle of the day. The few who did wander in were trim women in sweat suits, most likely mothers looking for a bouquet to brighten up their dining rooms or kitchens. They wandered around the shop, their arms across their chests, their heads craned in furtive positions above the Yankee candles in their thick glass jars outside the cooler—those bilious scents of Midnight Oasis, Garden Hideaway, Pink Lady Slipper. The mothers smiled sweetly at Hannah and the girls, and chose gerbera daisies or sunflowers. Hannah would check the cuckoo clock on the wall, and seconds later she would check it again as she waited for those tiny wooden doors to fly open and the chipped blue cuckoo to shriek. When her shift ended, she would at last loosen the strings of her apron and go for her jacket and handbag. She would drive off to pick up Janine by the bike racks outside the school library, Janine, who would tell her nothing about her day, who would only complain that she was starving or tired and just wanted to go home and would ask why Hannah hadn't scheduled Ethan's appointment for earlier. Why did Janine have to go too? Hannah would then pick up Ethan, who would drop his backpack on Janine's leg, and she would swat at him and then he at her, and they would bicker and snipe at each other until Hannah hollered at them: *Cool it, Jesus Christ, before I drive off the road with all your noise.* And on to the dentist's office, where the terse receptionist with the Boston accent presided over the waiting room, her jaw snapping a plum-size wad of bubble gum, always that syrupy smell of bubble gum and the cloying smell of fluoride, the high wheeze of the drills in the back room. Were people meant to turn off their senses every day of their lives? She would see that poster of the family with the identical pie-smiles, their teeth synthetically white. They sat with their arms around one another on a white porch swing, beneath them the words "Unleash the potential of your smile." Perhaps they were a real family. They looked alike, the brown-eyed, short-haired, strong-cheeked husband and wife. It was oddly believable that this athletic family had all decided to go get their teeth whitened (maybe Dad was a dentist) and, worse, have their photo taken to advertise this fact. Which led her to believe that if they had to be photographed—as if to prove a point—they could not have been happy.

What sort of person deconstructed a poster like this?

But it was just a consultation for Ethan and would not take all that long. She and Janine would sit rigidly beside each other while they waited, and eventually they would all head home, where Hannah would have to nag them to hang up their coats and leave their sneakers by the front door and not eat any chips before dinner, and then she would set a pot to boil for pasta, spaghetti of course, dreadful spaghetti, one of the few things they all agreed to eat. She had cooked spaghetti four hundred ways, three thousand times, and in the freezer sat a value pack of chicken breasts, two of which she would bread and fry up to serve along with the pasta. She would continue on as if on a conveyor belt, forward to dinner, forward to the dishes, to homework (after all, Janine's paper was due tomorrow) and the sound of Lovell coming up the front steps, later each night, and the kids demanding to watch TV or use their dad's computer (but had they finished their homework? Janine's paper?) and Lovell would say vacantly, *I need the computer tonight. I have hours of work to do.*

Jamie remained standing there in the same empty parking spot. The sky had gone gray now, and she could feel the gray, she was sure, settling onto her like heavy insulation, wrapping her tight. It was October, and soon would come winter, and Hannah thought of Marcy's bland smile and remembered that Lovell had a dinner meeting tonight, so he would return even later than usual, worn down, his mind full of numbers, last night's fight entirely forgotten.

The pickup edged forward. It had been nearly twenty years, two decades, since that moment when Doug had proposed to her. She was a cloud back then—she was air, she was sky, the sun and the moon. She had replied, "Yes, of course, of course," and he had kissed her and lifted her up and around. That moment, right then, eighteen years ago now—did it ever get any better than that?

Her foot rose and returned to the brake.

Chapter 23

One night, as a nor'easter blew in and the house shuddered against the wind, Lovell found Janine in the kitchen, her eyes on the computer screen in the dark of the room. Ethan had gone to bed an hour earlier. "What are you doing down here?"

"What does it look like?"

"How are you feeling these days?" Lovell asked her.

"I'm feeling awesome. Spectacular."

"Listen. Should we try to find another therapist for you guys?"

Predictably, she shook her head. "No. Talking to her or some other shrink is just dumb. It's not going to do anything to get Mom back. Jeff thinks it sounds like Dr. Valmer is putting feelings in our mouths. He's right—she tells us that 'it's normal to feel scared and sad.' He said I should try to talk about being angry, but when I tried that, she was all like, 'You're angry that your mom left and you have every right to feel that way,' and I kind of wanted to tell her to fuck off, that she didn't know shit about shit." She pushed her chair back from her computer and turned to him. Her hair had begun to grow in again. He really hoped she would let it grow longer this time.

"You don't feel scared and sad?" he asked. "You just feel angry."

"What was your and mom's wedding like?"

Where had this come from? "Well, it was on New Year's Eve," he said, but she already knew that. "The temperature was below zero outside, and all anyone talked about was the cold."

She appeared disappointed.

"Mom looked gorgeous. We had the ceremony at the church where she went as a kid, this quaint, old white building that looked out over the ocean. And the reception was at Grandma and Grandpa's house. We kept it small, maybe seventy or eighty people. Someone hung up little blue lights all around the living room. The band, they were friends of Mom's, and everyone danced until late." He thought a moment. "I even got Great-Aunt Irene to dance with me—"

"The one who weighs, like, three hundred pounds?"

"And Mom's cousin Monica."

"She lives in Spain?"

He nodded. "Everyone must have danced with everyone else. I think I even danced with Uncle Simon and my father. By the end of the night, your mom and I were so exhausted, we could barely stand up. The night before Mom had you, we were looking through the wedding album and remembering all this stuff, and then it seemed perfect that you arrived the next day. I remember saying that to her in the delivery room. I told her how much I loved her. And you. We couldn't keep our hands off you. You were so docile." He looked at Janine. "You're not going to offer to carry a baby for the neighbors."

"I'm still thinking about it," she said. "But they've put it on hold until Stephen's mother gets better. She had a stroke last week and has been in the hospital. I'm waiting until she's out before I say anything to them."

"Oh. OK."

"I wish Mom were here."

He nodded. "Me too."

"Right."

"Don't start this up again. She was my wife. Does that ever occur to you? We were married for almost sixteen years."

Janine stood, her hands in fists on her hips. "Do you ever feel a little bit guilty that maybe she went away that morning because she was fucking afraid of you? Because she wanted to escape?"

"Not this again," he said. "You are unbelievable."

"Well? You were horrible to her."

"We're done here."

"That's good, keep on denying everything. You are so full of shit," she said before she shut off the computer and stomped out of the kitchen.

He waited for the sound of the front door slamming, and in a moment, *crash,* there it was. She would march across the lawn and over the gulley and to the house next door to her confidants, her true loves, who were just waiting for her to come and pour out her sorrows to them so that they, this fun, hip couple, could console and comfort her in a way that he could not.

It was after ten. She should have been reading a book or getting ready for bed. To distract himself he set out his own laptop and scanned through the latest Pacific sea surface temperatures, the wind speeds from the northwest, waiting for her to return.

Hannah had asked him more than once whether all his charts and graphs, all his statistics—didn't they ever grow tiring? *Do you ever get sick of trying to predict the precise movement of every molecule in the atmosphere? When you look so close at something, doesn't it start to disappear? Doesn't it lose its fundamental it-ness?* "No," he had responded. "When you understand something, you see more, not less, of its essence. This 'fundamental it-ness,' or kinetic energy or pedesis or whatever you are actually talking about, is the basis of everything I do."

She had just shaken her head as if she thought he had misunderstood her questions.

One o'clock came, one thirty, and he decided to go to bed. Janine had stayed over next door once or twice before after watching movies. She would be back in the morning.

Chapter 24

The truck pulled ahead and was gone. Hannah waited alone at the exit. She saw a flash of something in the corner of her eye, and there was Jamie beside her window. She swallowed a balloon of air. He made a sympathetic face, and embarrassingly she began to cry. She had to turn away from him. Maybe this was how they would continue today, stop and start, forward and backward and forward again until—what?

When she finally got herself together, she looked back at him and he set his hands on his heart with genuine sympathy. She rolled down her window. "I don't know what I'm doing," she admitted.

A car pulled behind them, and he said, "Come on, Hannah. Turn around and park over there. Let's get you feeling better," and she did, if only to allow the other car behind her to drive by.

Once in the passenger seat again, he held her wrist and massaged her pulse. He stopped every few moments to adjust his pressure. Doug used to find her pulse on her neck and wrist, set his own pulse against hers as if trying to synchronize them.

Her tears soon began to slow. "You must think I'm crazy," she said at last. She pulled her hand back. "I don't know why I care. Do you meet women like this a lot? Do you just ingratiate yourself with strange women all the time?"

"Every day," he said.

She ran her fingers through her hair and squeezed at the roots.

"I can help."

She felt split into two halves, one glad for his words, the other too old and wary for promises like these. "So what now?" she asked.

"There are too many people here. There are too many of my students who could see me and just come right over here and bug us. Let's drive back to that other beach," he said. "We'll say our good-byes there." It was a relief to her, his acknowledgment that their time together deserved a notable good-bye, that she was worthy of this.

She pulled out of the parking lot and onto the one-way road that wound past the enormous, empty fields and then on toward Morrissey Boulevard.

"I'm wrung out today," she told him as she drove. "See what you've done to me?"

He set a hand on her knee. "But soon you'll be back in your store with all those flowers and you'll be just fine. And Lovell will be glad to see you after a long day at his office, won't he? And the kids? It'll be good to get back home, get back to life, won't it?"

Hannah recoiled inside at his obvious sarcasm. "What about you? Who's waiting for you at home?"

"I wish it were you," he said.

"Come on," she said, laughing. "Tell me the truth."

"I told you—I never lie."

He looked down at his fingers. He drew a deep breath and then another. He turned and glanced around the car, at the stained cup holder, up at the visors, at the backseat, the branch from that willow, Hannah's green work apron thrown in a heap. He reached for his backpack, and her heart skipped a beat, but he pulled out a bottle of water, just that, and downed a long gulp.

How strange that it was only a right turn, she remembered now, and you followed this road to that long, dusty parking lot at Carson.

A red-haired woman stood by as three young children chased a seagull across the sand. An old man helped a boy fly a yellow kite that caught a wind and spun in a dizzy circle as the man and boy struggled to hold the string. At the far end of the beach, a large family had set up a picnic and milled around a cooler.

"We'll go dip our feet in the water before you leave," Jamie said. "Just for a minute."

"It's October," she said. "That water is freezing."

"And?" he said.

"I'll stay back here and watch you."

The woman talked into her cell phone and briefly looked over at Hannah and Jamie. Hannah could now see that she was the children's sitter. The children had darker skin and smaller bones—and the woman had that bored, superior look of a full-time nanny. Two of the children began to dig a hole in the sand with their fingers while the third, a doll-faced girl with two long braids down her back, watched from the side.

Jamie kicked off his sneakers and walked toward the tide. He turned and waited for Hannah to do the same, but she shook her head. "I said I'm staying here," she called.

"Do I have to tell you again that I know what's best for you? Have you learned nothing today?"

She half smiled.

"Fine," Hannah replied, and she left her shoes and socks by a cracked clam shell. She stepped in just to her ankles. The frigid water stung her toes and seeped into the bottom of her pants, and she bent down to roll them up toward her knees. She turned to see if the nanny or anyone else on the beach was watching her, but the nanny had turned her back and the others were each occupied in some way.

"Here goes nothing," he said, and he charged toward the water. He clapped his hands together over his head and dove in cleanly, reemerging a moment later. He paddled several yards out, flipped over, and swam underwater, resurfacing just in front of her. "Come in," he said, and she shook her head and said, "You must be cold blooded."

He ducked beneath the surface again and tried to tug her down, but she managed to kick him away playfully. She felt a wet clump wash past her feet. A fish? Seaweed? The nanny, although she tried to hide that she was doing so, had turned back to Hannah and watched her shake her foot around.

Jamie swam next to Hannah and took her hand, and she felt his side drift against her leg, his slick, icy skin, and a charge in her chest, a quickening at the center of her stomach.

And then he stopped. He planted his fists into the muddy sand at the bottom of the water and pushed himself upright. He shook out his hair. "You're right. It's too cold."

Hannah followed him back toward the dry sand where his sweatshirt lay. She picked it up and held it out toward him. He ran a finger around the rim of her ear as if to remind her of the possibility that hovered between them. She moved her hand toward his stomach, but he flinched. "What was that?" he said.

Her face burned as she scanned behind him. The nanny was only a few feet away, picking up some trash that the kids had left. The grandfather and the boy were now winding the kite string back onto its reel, their backs to her.

Hannah stood with her damp, bare toes dug into the clumped sand. "I guess it really is time for me to go," she said.

He turned his eyes back to her. He was impossible to read. What did he even want from her today? "Play one quick game with me first. Let's play word association."

The grandfather and the boy dumped out a canvas tote bag of plastic digging toys and began a sand castle. "I'm worried about my children," she said. It was one thing she had over him, the one thing he could never understand, the pull of motherhood.

"OK. Kids. Resilient."

A current moved through her lungs. "Everyone needs a mother."

"Childhood. Your childhood, one word," he said, and he hooked a finger through one of hers. She pulled away and said, "Water."

"Breath," he said. "Breath, come on, your turn."

"Life," she replied.

He ran his finger down the soft inside of her forearm. She allowed herself to take in the sensation of being touched by someone she hardly knew, then pulled back again. "I said 'water' because I grew up on an island, Martha's Vineyard."

"Isolation?"

"Only in the winter. Absolute chaos in the summer. Tourist central."

"Skin," he said, lifting her hand to kiss her palm. "Salt." He turned to face her and curved his hand behind her neck and pulled her toward him. "Wait," he said against her forehead.

"I do not understand you," she said as she shoved him away. "What do you want from me?" She straightened her shirt. She glanced behind him and saw a plane descending, its red taillight blinking. She heard a faraway cough.

When in her other life had she finally lost her desire for the next moment and then the next? It seemed to have happened slowly, not in one sudden blow, but over thousands of ordinary minutes, in the tiniest of choices meant to lead her toward a well-defined future, the sort that had been chosen and lived by so many other people.

Jamie's watch read 2:06. "I'm leaving now," she said, although she was weighted, still not entirely ready to move. He nodded as if he knew exactly what she meant, even when she did not.

Chapter 25

At seven o'clock the next morning, Janine still had not returned. When Lovell went next door, Stephen told him that she had left their house about an hour earlier. "She said she was going back home. She told me she called you to say she was sleeping here last night." Lovell was not sure whether to thank him for befriending Janine or accuse him of essentially taking her away—for months, really—and now losing her. "Listen, I'll come over as soon as we hear anything from her," Stephen promised.

Back at home, Ethan had been watching TV for an hour now, but Lovell could not bear the silence that would come if he turned the thing off. He tried to sit and watch for a while but found himself staring at the clock. He finally called his mother, and she showed up soon after.

"Lovell," she said when he opened the front door for her.

"Janine should have her own cell." He led his mother inside the house. Janine shared a phone with Ethan, and it had been his turn this week.

"Let's think this through." Joanne set her brown shoulder bag on the table, went to him, and wrapped her hard arms around him. He let himself be held like this for as long as he could stand before gently backing away.

"I need to be doing more right now, something useful. I have to do something to help find her," Lovell said.

He called Janine's friend Stuart, but Stuart's mother answered and said that he was at his father's house. "And anyway, those two kids haven't hung out in a long time." Lovell tried the family across town, the Woodsons, whom Janine sometimes babysat for, but the mother knew nothing. He reluctantly tried Leah—Janine had been talking to her about interning at her company next month. "You don't know where she is?" Leah asked. "Jesus, Lovell."

"You think I'm not concerned? You don't think I'm a wreck right now?" He tried to regroup: "Maybe she went to her school for some reason."

"Will you keep me posted?" Leah asked. "I'm really worried."

"I am too," he snapped.

Ten o'clock came and Ethan had fallen asleep on the couch. Lovell left his mother with Ethan at the house while he drove around the neighborhood and other streets nearby, through the center of town, scanning the sidewalks for Janine. The winter sky was a dim slate color. The town appeared fairly abandoned on this cold day. A couple of women dressed in snow jackets chatted with each other as they headed into the post office, but no one else could be seen. Lovell scanned the empty parking spaces, the stores, which appeared empty as well. People were at work, of course. Children were in school. He drove around her school and Ethan's, back through town, around a few other neighborhoods, trying to imagine where else she might be, switching the radio from news to classical to rap, then finally just turning it off.

At eleven, Lovell decided to call the police, though he guessed that it was too soon to file a report. A gruff-voiced dispatcher answered. "Hang in there, dear. Don't worry. We'll file anyway. One of the guys will be there soon."

A squad car arrived minutes later with its lights flashing. The new chief, Russ Evans, and a young officer stood with Lovell on the front porch and helped him fill out the intake. The young guy, probably new, stood like a soldier, his back rod-straight, his head at attention. Lovell guessed that on the way here, Russ had provided at least a cursory history of the family.

Lovell explained that there had been a disagreement between him and his daughter. "She can get pretty overheated," he said. "And I—I mean, sometimes it's not easy. Anyway, she's stayed with the neighbors before, so I didn't think that much of it."

A woman who he thought might live down the street walked past, pushing a double stroller, glancing over at them.

"She mention anything about a favorite hangout with friends, some place she liked to go or anything?" Russ said.

Lovell grew warm. "We've been staying pretty close to home these days."

"Any guesses at all where she might have gone?"

Here were these questions again. He shook his head. "I called everyone who might know. I checked everywhere I could think of. I really can't imagine where she might be." He felt his face grow damp.

Russ seemed to understand or at least sympathize and clapped a hand around Lovell's arm. "Hard age." Lovell tried not to wince. It was unbearable to be touched by any of them right now.

"We're on it, Mr. Hall," the other officer said with the voice of someone young trying to sound older.

"Thank you," Lovell said. They said their good-byes and he stepped back inside. He turned to face his mother and Ethan, who were now standing by the small side table in the hallway. Ethan looked up at him, expectant.

"She'll come back. She'll be fine," Lovell said.

"You swear?"

"How about you and me go drive around town and look for her?" his mother said to Ethan. "It can't hurt, right? I'll buy you an ice cream, if you'd like."

"Good idea," Lovell said, grateful for this unexpected sensitivity, and he went for Ethan's coat. He watched while they headed out the door.

Leah showed up at the house soon after. "I can't work. I'm too upset. I still cannot believe that this happened and that I'm even standing here right now," she said.

He told himself to ignore the whiff of judgment that had always emanated from this person and her family, now that he thought about it.

The two made their way to the kitchen table, where they pretended to read the paper. Leah, a solid, long-faced woman who looked nothing like her sister, managed a venture capital fund that invested primarily in women-run companies. "My parents are coming over soon," she said after a while. "I hope you don't mind. They're really concerned too."

"That's fine," Lovell said. "It's still cold out there? Still snowing?" he asked, although he could see through the window that it was.

"It's freezing," she said.

"Janine doesn't even have a coat on."

Leah glared at him.

"She took off before I could give her one."

Leah just shook her head and checked her watch. "You have any wine or liquor? I don't care if it's too early to drink."

He half smiled, but she remained stony. He said, "I'll go find something."

His mother and Ethan eventually returned and peeled off their coats. "No luck," his mother said.

"You OK?" Lovell asked Ethan.

"I guess so," he said, and he went upstairs.

LATER THAT AFTERNOON, the doorbell rang. Hannah's parents stood holding hands on the front porch. "Lovell," Donovan said, and he promptly hid his face in his hands.

Lydia stepped past the two men into the house and gathered Ethan in her arms. She was a petite woman with a hushed contralto voice. Beneath her nut-brown coat, Lovell saw her double strand of pearls around her neck. Her style had not changed over the years. Her eyes were swollen now, and mascara dotted across one eyelid.

She gave Joanne a careful hug and squeezed Lovell's forearm. Lydia had always seemed unsure of what role she should assume with him. Mother? Friend? Peer?

A linebacker-size Irishman with a shock of white-blond hair, Donovan gave Ethan a bear hug, then stood back and wiped at his nose. "Remember," he said, "that fortune favors the brave. We'll get through this, we will."

THE PHONE RANG that afternoon, as they were tidying up the kitchen. It was a girl, and at first Lovell wondered whether she was calling for Janine. But then she introduced herself as Melissa Michaels, the victim advocate who had been assigned to him and his family. He walked the receiver upstairs to his bedroom and took a seat on his bed facing the window. He gathered a long breath before they began.

"I'm sorry for all that's happened to you, Mr. Hall," she said.

"Thank you." Did she know about Janine?

"So I need to tell you that there's been an arrest. The police picked up a man named James Trobec, who's wanted for two other murders."

"They found Hannah?"

"No, well, no, not yet." She paused for too long a moment. "So this man, he's Caucasian and he's from Somerville. He was working part-time at his brother's auto shop in East Cambridge and taking one class—Mechanical Engineering—at UMass Boston."

Lovell's mind spun. "What's the connection to Hannah?"

"I talked to a detective in Boston Homicide who's overseeing the case, and he said that the other two cases were women who fit profiles like Hannah's. They went missing for a while, and then some—this sort of evidence turned up, just, like, pieces of it. So they're considering him a possible suspect for Hannah too. Detective Ronson—that's the man who's got the case—he sent me the report." She cleared her throat. "This guy is forty-three and he has a wife and a young child. And they arrested him up near Bar Harbor late last night. He was picked up on speeding and a probable DUI." Lovell heard the sound of a page turning. "Are you OK?"

"Yeah," he said. "But, well, they don't know any more about Hannah, right? We still don't have a match on those things, those bones that turned up?"

"That's all the report says. I can try to find out more. Do you want me to call the detective and ask him?"

"All right."

"Are you sure you're OK, Mr. Hall?"

What was he expected to say? "Did they ever find her car?"

"I'm not sure. It doesn't say here."

"How is it possible for them to know so little? When will the DNA results come in?" he asked.

"I don't see anything in the report about that. I'll be sure to ask Detective Ronson."

Lovell stared out the window at the leafless trees motionless against the ice-blue sky. It had stopped snowing. Every single update that had come over the past three months had been an empty bombshell. "Can I talk to this detective?" Lovell finally said. "You have his number?"

"I'm supposed to be your primary contact, Mr. Hall."

"Just this one time. Please. Think of how this is for me."

New snow coated the backyard and had been blown by the wind into feathered patterns. The earth was beautiful and atrocious.

"HOW ARE YOU holding up?" Ronson asked that evening. He had some sort of an accent, maybe faded Irish.

"Fine," Lovell said. "I have some questions for you, if that's all right."

"Fire away."

"Melissa said this guy's wanted for a couple other similar things?"

"Yep."

"How were the women similar?"

"Ages, looks, circumstances. The first one was up in Maine, around Old Orchard. One of the others was in Southie too. You didn't see anything about Nikki Andrews a few years back? There was a good amount of press. Nice-looking lady. Nowhere near as much airtime as your wife, but the story got out there."

Lovell flinched. "I guess I don't watch the news all that much."

"Smart man," Ronson said. "So, what else have you got for me?"

"Are you absolutely sure that Hannah wasn't kidnapped and taken somewhere? Isn't that beach the place where all that mob stuff happened, where those bodies were found?"

"Yeah, it used to be one of Whitey's spots."

Lovell thought a moment. He would have to continue to be transparent throughout this process. "Did Detective Duncan tell you about our—that talk? The argument I had with Hannah on that last night?"

"He did," Ronson said. "It was good of you to come forward. I'm sure it was no easy thing to do. But I'd chalk the whole thing up to bad timing, Mr. Hall. Being angry at you didn't make her get in that car and drive to Southie and meet that guy, assuming that's what happened, of course."

"Right," Lovell said. A whole lot of assumptions were being made.

"You know, aside from this case, Southie isn't what it used to be. My niece just spent half a million on a condo—excuse me, *loft*—there. Carson's been cleaned up over the past few years."

"Huh," Lovell said. He had managed to sound both provincial and elitist.

"Anyway, her reason for going there might be the sort of thing that I call an irrelevant unknown. It seems like it should be a big part of the case, but once we've got enough evidence, we can set the question aside. It's just not important for the purposes of the prosecution. Don't beat yourself up over it." Ronson's tone changed. "So what else can I do for you?" It was a Boston accent. How had Lovell missed it? Maybe Ronson had masked it earlier. Maybe he himself lived in South Boston.

"The evidence. I guess that's my next question," Lovell said. "How much longer until you'll get the DNA identification on those bones?" He hated saying the words.

"How long has it been? Hold on a sec." Lovell heard the sound of typing. "Mid-November, mid-December? You should hear anytime now."

Chapter 26

But Hannah *had* loved: Baby Janine, her smell, vanilla and bananas, her miniature toes, her light furry hair, so much of it so soon. And as a toddler, her botched words ("Mum mum" for everything and everyone), her plush legs and stomach, her poreless skin, that she chewed grass and rocks and dandelions. The older Janine, her photographic memory, her unwittingly poetic observations about the world and her endless questions about the sky and her needing to have exactly the same three songs sung to her—"Hush, Little Baby," "Twinkle Twinkle, Little Star" and a short song that Hannah had made up about buttercups—before sleep each night. And Ethan as a baby, bigger and slower, but just as warm and easy to soothe, a deeper voice than Janine's, his blocky fists, his stubbier toes, his full-body wails and thrashing protests against any discomfort. As a toddler, he was happy to sit in the corner of a room stacking anything plastic, and then, remembering her, he would stumble to Hannah and lie across her lap for just a second, then return to playing. His wispy brown hair, his light eyes the same color as hers, his long, gangly legs even when he was as young as three and four, and as a child, his sweet gibberish at bedtime, his names for her—Me, Mima. And before her babies: Sophie, her perfume that smelled of ginger, the low-cut silk shirts that she wore even to the office, her unabashed femininity, her deep belly laugh. Of course Lovell was attracted to her. Who wasn't? The girls at the shop and their optimism, the way they barely touched the flowers, afraid to snip off too much stem, to lose even one petal—and when had she, Hannah, grown so careless? She hardly noticed the stems or the petals anymore. And earlier, much earlier, Doug of course, and there were smaller loves, and loves from a distance, and the love of her family, her mother's heels clicking down the hallway on her way from kissing Hannah good night; her father pretending to lose at thumb wrestling and the little motorboat called *Shy One*—after a Yeats poem—that he kept at Wasque. Leah and how she used to dress Hannah in her clothes and doted on her as a mother would. Grandfather clocks, Burdick's honey caramel truffles, antique glass perfume bottles, the smell of huckleberry, cantaloupe, jasmine. Emily Dickinson and her white clothing, her agoraphobia, her slant rhymes. Fenway Park at twilight, the Green Monster, the greasy hot dogs, and the watery beer. Mexico, Tunisia—Tunis and its colors, its bleached light, Lovell's body against hers when she felt as if she might not make it. She still loved flowers. She did. Orchids, gerbera daisies, cornflowers and ranunculus and snapdragons and sweet peas and waxflowers. She still loved how just handing flowers to any decent human being made the person smile—hadn't she said this to Lovell just the other week? And Lovell, this man, her husband: there were corners and moments, slivers and sometimes more, safety and comfort and ease and acceptance and family and loyalty, and these were all things to love.

"Childhood," Hannah said to Jamie. "Yours now. One word."

The grandfather glanced over at them.

"Oh, yawn, here we go." Jamie grabbed the stick from her and whacked it against the sand.

"Mine," she said. "I was surrounded by beaches. My family loved me. And adolescence—I think it's all about the other kids, you know, whether they see you or don't. The girls who are invisible have the hardest time. People are at their most superficial at fifteen, right? Nothing matters but appearance. I didn't have too much to complain about."

"Do you now?"

She shrugged, her eyes on the sand.

"But doesn't it feel good not to know? For the first time in your life, not to know what is going to happen right now? And now? And now?"

She began to chew the edge of her thumbnail.

"Tell me why you really came here today."

She took a seat on the sand and draped her hands over her knees. "I didn't know where else to go."

The grandfather and the boy had finished their sand castle.

She would go home now. After the dentist, she would pull the car into her driveway and herd the kids inside. Dinner, homework, Lovell's always-overdue return home, and later on she would follow him as he lumbered upstairs and into their bedroom, and she would change into an old T-shirt, and by the time she took her place on the left half of the mattress, his breathing would have slowed and the snoring would start up, quietly at first, and there she would find herself, alone, waiting for sleep to come as she did each night. She would look up through the window at this overcast sky, this same sky that she sat beneath now, and she would wonder what might have happened if she had stayed just a few more minutes on that beach.

Chapter 27

The next day, Hannah's sister and parents, as well as Lovell's mother, came to the house again. Joanne set out a tub of chocolate rugelach and a small barrel of pistachios from Costco. Hannah's mother unwrapped a wedge of cheddar and placed it beside a fan of paper-thin crackers that she had arranged across a plate. "I brought something for Ethan," she said, pulling a copy of *The Two Towers* from her purse.

They took turns searching the surrounding towns for Janine, waiting by the phone, and trying to make small talk. Ethan came and went nervously from his bedroom. Lovell thought to do an Internet search for James Trobec and those women. He thought to do a search for Detective Ronson and try to find out what other cases he had handled and how they had gotten solved, but Lovell stopped himself before turning on his computer. It would be better to avoid any information with the potential to be emotionally destabilizing right now. First he had to find Janine.

Lovell noted that no one touched any of the food, and finally he walked the plate and the tub of rugelach around to each of them. "We've got to eat," he said sadly to Donovan.

Late in the afternoon, the Munroes left, and shortly after, so did Lovell's mother, telling him to be in touch and contact them as soon as he heard anything. On the way, she squeezed his arm out so tightly that he flinched.

THAT EVENING, LOVELL sat by himself in the kitchen, a plow groaning down the street outside. It was a relief, if a small relief, to finally be alone. He no longer had to tiptoe around, aware of his every word and expression in the face of Hannah's family. He could breathe. He could panic.

He understood that all day he had kept control of a small burn inside him. But it had grown and spread despite his best efforts. It had filled his whole body and was impossible to contain any longer. *Goddamn* Janine for doing this to him. Did she ever give one thought to how her disappearance might affect him? Men were always the ones criticized for lacking empathy. What a fucking joke that was. He had allowed Janine to shave her head, if that was what made her feel better about everything; he had driven the kids, week after week, to a therapist a good forty-five minutes away; he had let Janine pal around with a couple of grown men instead of insisting that she make some friends her own age; hell, he had listened calmly while she announced her asinine idea to carry their child. Plenty of fathers—and mothers—would not have been a fraction as accepting or supportive as he had been.

Her viola lay next to her bow on the floor in the corner of the room, the black case nowhere to be seen. It had cost him over $1,400, and here it sat, tossed onto the floor like an old notebook. He had wanted to buy a used viola, but of course Hannah would not have it. Those secondhand instruments that they had seen in the store were "scratched and ugly and completely lacking artistry, you know?" she had said. "They all look like they came flying out of the same machine."

He reached down and picked up Janine's hand-carved viola. He held it before him by the slim wooden neck. He tightened his grip around the strings and fingerboard. *You think you know hardship? You think you know devastation and loss and total emotional abandonment—and hatred—you think you really know that?* he could say to them. He could snap this thing in half without even trying. He could show her what true misery really looked like.

He had thrown that perfume bottle on the bathroom floor and then he had crushed it again and again because he could no longer stand the image of Hannah's disgusted face in the other room, the unbearable noise that her loathing drilled into his head. She could not even stand to look at him. When was the last time she had even looked at him? He had pounded his fist into one wall and another and smashed his foot into the door and the toilet and cabinet. He kicked the wall and smashed his fist into the door. He wanted it gone, her disgust, the sight of her back to him, the picture of her with Doug, her endless disappointment, Sophie, the fucking flower store, Leah, Lydia, the estate on the Vineyard, all of it gone. He marched back into the bedroom, and she accused him of being patronizing when he was really nothing but a "loser," and he went toward her and kicked the bed frame and reached forward to punch her.

The memory came to him from nowhere.

Janine flashed by in the hallway, and he had gone to shut the door so she would not have to see any more, and then he had returned to Hannah, his fingers hot by his side. She held her arms tight around herself and made herself small. He slammed a fist against the heel of his other hand. She stared up at him, stunned.

But he stopped himself. He had never hit her before. He had never hit anyone, and this person about to lift a fist to his wife, this man raging—this animal—was not him.

Lovell had dropped his arm, and at last, for the briefest moment before they resumed hurling terrible words at each other, there had been quiet inside him.

The bottle of perfume had not fallen on its own. He had come within one millimeter of destroying her. The plow outside continued to groan. A dog barked. Janine was out in that world somewhere.

He was a pitiable, angry boy. He had been a terrible, hateful husband, a mediocre father.

Chapter 28

At nine the next morning, the doorbell rang. Two policeman stood behind Janine in the blinding sunlight.

Lovell brought his hands to his mouth.

"She was sleeping on the Boston Common."

"She was?"

Janine stood there on the front stoop in her ratty gray sweatshirt and jeans, her face chapped, a small bruise next to her eye. Her hairline was irritated and pink. Her hands were covered in dirt. A line of icicles glistened from the side of the front porch's overhang. She had slept outside in this brutal winter weather—he did not want to imagine what might have happened to her. Lovell reached for her. "Thank you," he said to the men. "Do you need anything from me?"

They shook their heads and turned to go.

She stepped inside, walked down the front hall, and scanned the living room, taking in Ethan on the couch. She only shook her head and trudged upstairs.

Lovell hurried up the stairs after her and pounded on her bedroom door.

"I don't want to talk," she called.

"You don't have a choice, my dear," he said. He pounded harder. The walls shook. "Open up this goddamned door, Janine."

"No."

"I swear, I will go get a hammer and I will knock this thing down if you don't."

"Stop it, Dad. Just please cut it out," she yelled. He thought he heard her begin to cry.

"Janine, I mean it." He pounded again on the door. He had to take her to the hospital and get her checked for frostbite and God knew what else. His heart beat in his throat. "You have to open this door."

"I'm scared," she yelled back. "OK? I'm fucking scared of you right now."

He blinked fast.

"Go away, all right?"

He stood there, with no sense of what to do or say. Of course she was scared. "Sweetie," he tried.

"What? What the hell do you want?"

"OK. All right. No more pounding." He tucked his hands around his sides. He waited there, but she said nothing. "You've been gone for two days. We need to talk. It's me here. It's just Dad." He thought he sounded better now. "I want to make sure that you're all right."

"No more yelling? No hitting anything?"

"No more," he promised.

Finally she pushed open the door and let him in. She walked toward the opposite corner of the room and he lowered himself onto her green beanbag chair. "Can you please tell me where exactly you've been?"

"Those cops just told you."

"I mean why you went to Boston and what the hell you were doing there and why—why you slept overnight in a god-damned park?"

"Stop being so mad. You said you'd try. You look like you're about to do something to me." Her voice had grown faint.

"I'm not," he said. He sighed. He let his body sink down into the beanbag chair. Hannah had once told him to use his words. "Instead of storming off, instead of throwing a book, why don't you use your goddamned words, Lovell?" This had only made him significantly more angry. He looked at Janine, pacing back and forth beside her music stand. He noticed a small rash above her ear. He said, "Someday I hope your daughter runs away and you feel a fraction of what I feel right now."

"Do you want to know more or not?"

"Yes. Keep going."

"Don't be mad."

"I won't."

"You will. You are."

He felt his forehead tense. He clenched his jaw. "I am doing the best I can."

"*Fine*. The other morning I was going to come home, but—" She lay down on her stomach across her bed, facing him. "Stephen and Jeff are moving to Montreal," she said, as if this explained everything. She swiped her hand across her nose.

"Oh?"

"I did it. You know, I offered to, you know, help them."

He swallowed hard. Stephen might have told him about this part when Lovell went next door looking for her.

"And they said no. They didn't even take me seriously for one minute."

"Janine. Sweetie." He nearly laughed with relief. "Why didn't you tell me?"

"Because it was fucking embarrassing, Dad. Could you be any thicker?"

"It was embarrassing to be turned down by two gay men?" She began to weep.

"I'm sorry. I'm sorry. Do you—" he began, "do you want to tell me what happened?"

"Some old friend of theirs up in Montreal is going to carry the baby for them. She's already *pregnant*. And now Jeff got a job up there and they're going to sell their house because she wants to be a part of the baby's life, and I guess they're totally fine with that, even though I told them it was a fucking horrible idea. What if she changes her mind and wants to keep the baby—because she doesn't have any other kids, you know?"

Lovell tried to take it all in. "Maybe you can visit them up there?"

"It won't be the same. And I got an e-mail that said I didn't make regionals. I'm going to quit viola."

He carefully set his hands on his knees. In five years, she would no longer be a teenager, and maybe, hopefully, these histrionics would subside. It was not soon enough. "I'm not sure what you want me to say right now."

"Definitely not that."

"Can you tell me why you went to Boston?"

"I don't know."

"You mind expounding on that one?"

"If you stop sounding like a dick."

He inhaled through his nose. He had no choice but to step carefully here if he wanted her to keep talking. "Deal."

"I was gonna take the train to Boston, but then it already left when I got to the station, so I just kept walking and then I went to Leland."

"Elementary?"

"Yeah."

"Why?"

"I just felt like it. I stayed there for a while and watched the kids at recess and the teachers and everyone. I kept thinking about when I went there and I started viola and was in that school play—you remember, I had to play a rat in *The Pied Piper*?"

"I remember painting whiskers on your face." He was not always an absent father. It had been only a few years since he'd begun to work evenings and weekends. He and Hannah had sat in the front row of Leland's cafetorium and snapped pictures of their daughter, the rat, marching in a line of other rats across the small stage. He had memorized her one line in the play, in case she got stage fright or forgot it. He sat at attention, ready to whisper up to her if she needed the help.

"And Mom made my costume, I think—that one out of those brown footie pajamas?"

Lovell nodded.

"Anyway, then I just walked around town and thought about stuff. I went to the library and read for a while. I read some Emily Dickinson poems. I went to Mom's store. It looks exactly the same."

"Does it?" he said, his heart dropping. "Weren't you cold?"

"Freezing."

"So why didn't you just come home?"

"Well, then I caught another train into Boston."

"Why?"

"I thought about going to Carson. I've never been there—we've never even been to South Boston, have we? But then on the train I got kind of freaked out by the whole idea, so I got out at Copley and I met a couple of kids who live at a shelter and they snuck me in and let me sleep there so I wasn't outside. But I had to be out early the next morning so no one would find out. I walked around there and Chinatown for a while. Whenever I got too cold, I went inside a store. I couldn't remember where anything was in Boston—I thought about trying to find Symphony Hall or the library. I went to the T to look at the map, but some freak started whispering to me and saying shit about his son, so I just left and went back outside and walked around more. And that night, I tried to find those kids again, but I couldn't, so I went in and out of the stores again and then I went back to the Common and then I guess I just fell asleep on a bench. And then these two cops are poking me and asking me all these questions.

"You don't need to give me a lecture about why this was all a dumb idea, Dad. I can see that you want to."

"Fair enough." He looked over at her bloodshot eyes, the charcoal smudge just below one eyebrow. "How did you get that bruise?"

"What bruise?"

He drew a deep breath. "Can I sit next to you?"

"No."

"I thought I might fall apart," he said. "When I realized that I didn't know where you went. I really felt it—everything inside me going haywire. My heart and my lungs and my stomach. I felt like every part of me might just explode." As he said it, he understood how true it had been. He may never have said anything like this before. It felt strange but good, a little like trying on someone else's clothes and seeing that they fit. "I could not handle it if you had been gone for one more minute. You might have come home and found that your dad was just a pile of organs on the floor."

"You're so fucking weird." She half smiled.

He looked over at her again. "You'll make other friends after Stephen and Jeff move." Hannah would know what to say right now. More importantly, she would know what not to say. "And if you want to try another instrument, that's fine."

"This is not about viola. Shit."

He waited for her to elaborate. She lifted the small pillow over her face. After a moment, she said, "I have so much homework to send in to school tomorrow. I'm going to be up all night."

"Can I help?"

"No. It's English."

"I speak English, you know." *Don't you know,* he nearly said, *don't you know that if I could, I would force those two men to stay next door—at least until you were ready for them to go?*

Chapter 29

A few nights after Janine had returned, Lovell found his banjo at the top of the metal shelving unit in the basement. He set out a folding wooden chair, rested his feet on an old recycling bin, and ran his fingers over a few strings.

He had never been all that good. But the metal strings against his fingers and that plinky sound had always activated some part of his brain that he probably otherwise never used. His mother had bought him a Gold Tone Cripple Creek when he started college, despite his father's pressing him to stay with the piano. He took banjo lessons from a woman in Somerville for a while, but a couple of years later, when he moved into the apartment in Brighton with Paul, he sold the instrument as well as his mountain bike for rent money.

Hannah had never heard him play and had asked him about

it every so often over the years. "Why not go buy a cheap one somewhere? I think it might be fun for you," she had said.

"Maybe," he had always said, but he never did.

A few years back, she bought him one for his birthday and insisted he play a song for her and the kids that same evening after dinner. They watched him strum and pick and fiddle with the tuning pegs, embarrassed as he tried in vain to remember those chords. Nothing came back to him. Not one chord or technique, not one position. "Come on," she said. "It doesn't have to be perfect. Just try any song." He finally managed a sorry version of "Skip to My Lou" before setting down the banjo. "Some other time," he said.

The boiler moaned. The room was unbearably hot, its windows bolted shut now for years. It was a mess down here. A corner of the carpet was rotted and black, possibly moldy, and there were a couple of huge boxes of broken tools that had to be fixed or just thrown away. Garbage bags stuffed with clothes that the kids had outgrown sat nearby. In another corner of the basement sat several boxes of Hannah's belongings, one full of her antique perfume bottles packed in newspaper, another with old photo albums.

He set the banjo back on the shelf and began to scrub caked dirt from the concrete floor, stack the shovels and ice scrapers, untangle and wind hoses. He worked until he felt a stinging between his shoulder blades. He headed upstairs and, after a tall glass of water, returned downstairs to vacuum the moldy carpet. He sliced into it with a knife, cutting away the black, rotted spots and stuffing them into garbage bags. He made a pile of rusted and broken tools to be thrown away.

He took a seat in an old rocking chair in the corner of the room. He considered all the tasks that remained before him: the stack of old blankets and sheets that had lain in a heap by the washing machine for a good decade now and would have to be washed; the boxes of gardening guides and travel books about France and Greece; the plastic crate full of poetry books, which would all need to go somewhere at some point. The seat of the chair sagged beneath him. He shifted his weight forward so as not to break it further. It had been Hannah's chair, where her nanny had rocked her so long ago, the same rocking chair where Hannah herself had held and fed both Janine and Ethan when they were young. "Nanny? You actually had a nanny?" Lovell had asked Hannah when Lydia first brought the rocking chair to this house.

He brushed a clump of dust now from the arm of the chair. He gathered the grubby blankets and sheets and carried them upstairs to the washer.

THE KIDS WERE asking to go back to school. Ethan missed his friends. Janine was tired of having to mail in homework. Lovell was torn: They needed to get back to life. They all did. But those DNA results could come in at any time. "Soon enough, you can go back," he told them.

In the days after Janine's return, a weight had begun forming within Lovell, a gravitational force born of his finally allowing a now undeniable probability to enter his mind. There was a chance that the lab would find another woman's DNA in those bones, but there was a greater chance that they would not.

Each day, he could feel himself hunkering down a little more, his body nearly solidifying in preparation for what would likely come. He could hear himself speak in a quieter, gentler voice to the kids. He kept the radio on low most of the time to fill the stark quiet. It was good to tend to their environment in these ways, to create a protected zone of comfort and warmth for them. For the first time in months, he felt as if he were kneeling down, keeping still on a raft that seesawed and bucked over ferocious water, holding steady and firm.

He cooked them soup one night, a minestrone from an old family recipe, and as they sat behind their bowls at the kitchen table, he looked over at his kids and said, "We are a family still," although he could not quite say just what he meant.

Ethan said, "What else would we be?"

Lovell exchanged a look with Janine, who said, "Just say, 'You're right, Dad.'"

"'You're right, Dad,'" Ethan echoed.

After dinner, Lovell went for the scrapbook that they had made with Dr. Valmer. "Come take a look with me?" he suggested, and with some hesitation, each took a seat beside him on the couch. Maybe it would look different to him now, less treacly. Maybe looking at it together could get them talking about some of the happier times.

He opened to the page that had Ethan's elephant-shaped card, the postcard Hannah had sent to Janine at sleepaway camp. He flipped back to the first page, "Our Mother," with the list of words below: *Thoughtful. Nice. Loved flowers. Pretty.*

"I hated making this thing," Ethan said.

"You did?" Lovell asked.

"Well, we didn't know what was going on, and Dr. Valmer made us act like we did."

"Plus," Janine added, "what about all the other things that we could have said about her? What about how even though she liked to cook, it stressed her out? What about how she always complained about the crowds at Fenway, you know, those meatheads everywhere who chugged beer and the ones who fell on top of her? I wanted to put in something like how she always nagged me to stand up straight and stop chewing my hair. Where was the page for that? And how about how anal she was about us keeping our rooms clean?"

"She used to yell at me for watching too much TV," Ethan added. "She told me I should ride a regular bike instead of my unicycle. She said it wasn't safe."

Lovell thought about it. Ethan had hardly ridden his unicycle since she had disappeared. He used to spend hours on the thing. "She was a good mother," Lovell said.

"Yeah," Janine murmured.

He thought to say more, maybe about how much she had loved them, or to make denials or jokes or resolutions or apologies—anything not to have to sit here with these children and listen to this silence. But none of the choices were quite right.

"I just thought the scrapbook was really stupid," Ethan said at last.

"A total crock of shit," Janine added.

Chapter 30

On the first day of February, Lovell woke to the sound of the doorbell. He bolted out of bed, threw on a bathrobe, and hurried downstairs before the kids woke. He heard the slamming of a car door outside somewhere, and as he stepped down the front hallway toward the door, he saw a news van pull up across the street behind another. Rain was pouring down outside. The sky was a murky gray. He had to do this. Once again, he had to open this door and let in something or someone with the potential to ruin them. He had no choice but to open the door right now.

On the front steps stood a girl, probably in her late teens or early twenties. She introduced herself as Melissa Michaels. She stood clutching the padded straps of a maroon backpack, her black bangs soaked and dripping. Standing here before him, she looked young enough to be his daughter.

They huddled on the porch to avoid the wind-driven rain. He did not want to invite her in. He did not want Janine or Ethan to come downstairs and see her here.

She adjusted her backpack and looked up at him before she spoke. "I'm sorry to have to tell you this, Mr. Hall." She kept her gaze on the hair at his forehead. "The DNA results for the arm just came in," she said. "Detective Ronson asked me to tell you that we can wait and not tell the news people yet, if you want."

"Shit." He bent forward and set his hands on his knees to steady himself. "Yeah. Please, yes, let's wait, if you don't mind."

"I'm really, really sorry," Melissa said, wiping raindrops from her glasses.

"The tests, they're definitive?"

She nodded gently.

"Shit," he said again. Ethan was just nine years old. Janine was only fifteen. And Hannah. Thirty-nine.

"Do you want me to stay?" Melissa gestured toward the door.

"Maybe just a minute." He knew he should invite her in.

She edged forward as if to hug him but then stepped awkwardly back. He wondered whether he was her first case.

He could hardly ask her to remain out here in the rain much longer, neither of them saying anything. He finally said, "OK."

"I think Detective Ronson said he would contact you. The trial date hasn't been set yet. But I'll let you know when it is. I'll call you." She repeated, "I'm—I'm so sorry."

The rain began to gust and trill around them. He looked down at her black rubber boots. He would remember these boots, he knew. If he passed them in a store or on someone else on the street, they would send him right back to this moment.

"Good-bye," she said.

"Good-bye, Melissa."

He watched her walk away and step into her car. He saw her sit for a moment behind the steering wheel, her head down, before she pulled her seat belt across her chest and turned on the ignition, shifted into reverse, and slowly pulled out of the driveway. A policeman waved aside another news van pulling up in order to let her pass. Lovell watched her car drive slowly down the street, breaking to avoid a squirrel, and finally disappear.

"Good-bye," he heard himself say again.

He wondered how long he could stand here on his front porch facing the reporters, getting drenched by the rain, before Janine or Ethan would come outside and ask him what was wrong.

Chapter 31

Later, he considered the not insignificant amount of will and bravery that it took to walk back inside that house, wake the kids, deliver the news to them, call Hannah's mother and father, her sister, Sophie, his own parents, everyone in the world, it seemed. He granted a few interviews with reporters, and this time he let himself say whatever came into his head: "How does this feel? It feels like fucking hell on earth, if you can't guess for yourself." Let them bleep out what they needed to.

Of course, what option was there but to tell everyone what had happened? Go back in his house, get his keys, and drive away from his kids and his life? It certainly crossed his mind.

He had done pretty well, he thought. He had held it together while the kids sobbed against him. He had invited Hannah's family to come to the house so that they could be together. He had extended an open invitation to Sophie as well, if she wanted to come and see the kids. And later, he had taken some time to himself in the bathroom to stare into the mirror and splash water on his face and hold the bottle of her lemongrass hand cream to his chest and say, "I'm sorry, I'm sorry, I'm sorry." To sit inside the empty bathtub and fold his huge body into itself, the bottle still in his hands, and say, "I'll do better. I will love them better. I will love them so much."

He had jumped headfirst into a massive, rocky canyon and was somehow still in one piece.

AFTER THE FUNERAL service at the church, once the kids returned to school, the day before Lovell went back to work, he stood in line to check out at Stop and Shop. He looked over, above the gum and candy, at a small TV showing the news. There was Susan Sperck saying Trobec's name. Lovell instinctively raised his hand to cover his eyes. He went to turn his cart and move to another aisle, but for some reason he stopped himself. He turned his eyes back to the TV. Trobec was seated across from Sperck in his oversize orange coveralls. His voice sounded younger than Lovell might have expected, higher and thinner, as if its lower register had been shaved away. Susan asked some questions about his life as a husband and father and then directed the conversation toward the inevitable. Trobec admitted that he had killed Hannah Hall and the other women, of course he had, and he supposed that he did regret it. "Especially now that I'm sitting here in this shit house."

Lovell considered grabbing the TV and hurling it to the floor. He was dizzy as the woman at the register checked out his groceries. He felt sickened as he slid his credit card through the machine.

After Melissa had left his house that day, Lovell's questions had nagged at him, despite what he now knew. In what way and to what degree and at what points had he himself contributed to her each and every move that day? It was excruciating to think about all those possible images, the words that may or may not have been spoken. He tried to imagine what she had seen and heard, what she must have thought, her memories and fears. The unthinkable fear.

Was it penance that he was after? A form of retroactive witnessing, the accompanying presence, himself there with her, if in hindsight, watching and promising to remember? Maybe it was a form of self-punishment. Maybe, but also proof that those "irrelevant unknowns" were in fact relevant. If they had not mattered to the police or Trobec or the lawyers, they certainly mattered to her—and to him. After all, these were the last moments of her life.

In the parking lot of the grocery store, something inside him began to loosen, a rock-hard knot that had pulled and twisted within him for months now. There were moments of her last day that he could or would not fathom. He understood that at some point he would have to let those parts go. He would have to leave them to her, because in the end, all of it was hers and hers alone, October 4, 2007.

Chapter 32

Jamie fished around inside his backpack. He pulled out a Swiss Army knife.

"Jesus," she said.

"I'm not going to hurt you. Here, you take it," he said, handing it to her. Better she have it than he, she supposed. "Open it," he said. "Pick one of the knives or the saw and pull it open."

She looked at him. Her mouth grew dry.

"Here," he said. He stuffed his hands under himself. "See? No hands. You be in charge."

She dug her fingernail into the groove of a long, thin blade and lifted it, but immediately pressed it back inside.

"Pull it out again," he said. "You choose some part of me, my arm or leg or chest."

"I don't think so," she said.

"All right, I'll pick." He looked down at his feet. "Here, my left leg." He lifted himself off his hands and leaned his knee toward her. He took her hand and directed it toward his calf. "Now touch me with the blade. Just for a second." Together, they tapped the flat of the knife to his skin.

"Again," he said, "but this time, leave it there. See what you can do."

He moved her hand toward him again, and she continued in this way, touching him with the knife, holding it against his skin for seconds longer each time. She had no idea what would happen, whether she would slip and cut him or whether he would grab her hand and turn the knife on her. There was, as he had promised, some horrible thrill to the weight of the knife in her hands, the warmth of his leg now against hers, and the way that he at once guided her hand and allowed her to choose the amount of pressure she exerted—this not knowing what she could or would do.

"Now turn it," he said.

She twisted the blade and brought it back to his leg. He nodded her forward, and she hoped that her trembling was not visible to him as she tried, with as little force as possible, to touch his skin without nicking it. But a line of red appeared below his knee and formed a trickle that rushed down his leg.

"I'm sorry," she said, and she set the knife on the sand. "No more."

"I barely felt that." He scooped up the drop with the pad of his thumb. "You sure you want to stop?"

"Yes," she said. She wiped up the rest of the blood on his ankle with the back of her hand. "What is this? What are you doing?"

He reached for the knife. "I want you to try again, and this time, make it hurt."

She tried not to show any emotion. She stood and carried the knife toward the water, but he raced to catch up with her. "That's not yours," he said. He snatched the knife and he dropped it inside his backpack. "Don't be ungrateful," he said. His face darkened. He was finally tired of her and tired of the back-and-forth between them.

"I'm going," she said.

He dropped the backpack on the sand. He suddenly looked hideous, a feral thing let out of his cage.

A heaviness dropped from her head through her chest, a brick of nauseating recognition of all that faced her now—and all that had faced her from the moment she first saw him. Everything that she had chosen not to see.

He nodded at her as if he could read her thoughts. He was ready now.

She had made an enormous mistake. She wanted Ethan and Janine and Lovell—she wanted them, she missed her family for the first time in so long. She wanted her mother and father, her sister and friends and everyone she had ever known. She wanted everything about her life. Was driving here and meeting this person the only way that she could have come to this?

But maybe she could still leave. She knew that she had to at least try. Her bare feet planted at the edge of the bitter water, she measured herself against him. She was nearly his height, but slighter, of course. He had a compact strength like a runner's, a leanness and force that she did not. But she had to try to escape. She would trick him in some way—and she had thought to try, and this itself was progress, an agreement or a decision at least, one with herself. If she was able to leave now, she would forever think back to the decision she had made on this day and the fortitude that she was able to gather.

She would have to wait until he had turned around or was otherwise occupied and she could get a few seconds on him before she ran.

His leg had begun to bleed again, three discrete lines that ran from the side of his knee to just above his ankle. Her pulse thumping in her ears, she knelt before him and licked her thumb, trying to steady her hand. "Here," she said, wiping away each line from the bottom toward the top, unsure of what she should do next, only that she had to keep on. "You should put pressure on those." She looked around them for rope or even seaweed that could be used as a tourniquet.

"I'll be fine," he said. "*You* try now."

"Me?" And then she understood what he meant. "No."

"You just start slow, like we did with me. You just barely touch your skin."

She saw herself as if from above, recoiling and thereby allowing him to direct her every move again. She forced herself to lean down and take the knife away. "Fine. Me. Here we go." She pulled out the blade. The blood in her arms and legs, her face and back, seemed to thicken and warm with the thought that she was here, she was in fact here on this beach. She was here with this person. He remained a few feet from her, watching with a new impatience as she tapped the blade against her forearm. He nodded her on—"Keep going, Hannah"—and she turned the knife, and it took the slightest pressure, barely any, the smallest sting, to produce a sprig of blood.

Three short lines, just as she had given him, and then he grabbed the knife back, folded it shut, and shoved it into his pocket. "All right, come on," he said, and he yanked her upright. He pulled her forward by her wrist. Three men wearing paint-spattered clothes leaned against a black van in the lot, and Jamie nodded at them as if in some kind of complicity. They stamped out cigarettes with their work boots and stepped back inside the van and were gone. The only car left in the lot now was hers.

Jamie shoved her back toward her car, his hand crushing her wrist, and with his other hand he opened the door and fumbled around in her backseat. He grabbed the willow branch and kicked the door shut, his hand still clamped around her wrist.

"Stop. Don't. Please, don't," she said, but he pushed her across the lot and over the curb and again toward the water.

She turned back to the parking lot. No cars drove on the

road behind them, no one else walked along the beach. He knocked her down next to a rotted old pier where the water rumbled in low waves. She struggled upward but he held her against the rocky sand, and just before he kicked her down under the wood slats, she was able to say, "Good-bye," to the sand, to her children and Lovell and her mother and father and sister. In her last moment, Hannah looked up and saw a faint pinkish-white cloud in the sky shaped like an orchid. Smog, maybe.

Chapter 33

Lovell locked up the house and stepped outside. The March air was breezy but warm and he tilted his face to the sky for a moment and soaked in the sunlight. Across the street, a woman he didn't recognize held a baby to her shoulder and buried her face against its head. She lifted her eyes and looked over at Lovell once, then again. He tried not to hide his face. He managed to actually wave to her.

He wandered next door to find Janine and the neighbors in their driveway. Stephen and Janine leaned side by side against the bumper of a U-Haul truck and snapped bottle caps into an icy puddle. The men would leave the next day, and within a couple of weeks, apparently, another family would move into their house. Janine kept her eyes on the puddle. Last week, she had gone to get her tongue pierced, but she had gotten too nervous and backed out in the end. A few days ago, she had dyed her hair, the little that remained, a pale purple. In some strange way, it suited her.

Jeff appeared in a black T-shirt and jeans. "Hey there," he said to Lovell, giving him a warm slap on the back. Stephen moved next to his partner and set his head on his shoulder. Here were two men in love, two people who unquestionably belonged together.

"You'll come meet Hannah?" Jeff asked Lovell.

He blinked.

"Janine didn't tell you? The name was her idea."

"It's a girl?" Lovell managed.

"It is. She—will be."

Janine said, "And Rose will be the middle name."

"Hannah Rose," Lovell said, glancing over at her. "Hannah Rose," he said again. He was grateful that the men had given Janine at least this. "Of course we'll come meet her."

Ethan wandered over and began to kick his soccer ball toward them. Lovell stopped the ball with his foot and reached down for it. He went to Janine and held her to his side before she pulled away. Ethan ran toward him and grabbed the ball from his hands.

Janine began to dance from side to side, and said to Jeff, "You promised you'd run through 'Humoresque' and 'The Swan' with me before you left."

All this time, Lovell had forgotten that Jeff was a cellist.

Stephen said, "You want to come hear them play at our house? It's empty, but we could sit on the floor."

Lovell looked at Janine, who only shrugged. "You go. Ethan and I will catch up with you later. Good luck with everything, guys." He shook their hands and said good-bye.

He turned toward his son, and the two kicked the soccer ball back and forth, back and forth, as they made their way in the newly spring morning across the gulley between the houses, across his patchy front lawn, and forward to their home.

LOVELL POURED DETERGENT into the machine in the basement, let the lid drop with a bang, and turned the knob. He listened while the machine filled with water and began to churn. It was late on the second night of April, nearly midnight, but he had awoken just now, remembering that Janine had a concert the next day. Her black skirt and white blouse had been sitting in the laundry basket in the basement for a week.

He would have to wait around until the washer cycle finished in order to dry the clothes in time for tomorrow morning. He paced the basement and considered getting his computer and doing some work. But he decided not to, decided instead to stay down here and see if he could find the box that he had tried but failed to find before, the cardboard box that contained the heavy glass tea set and hand-stitched djellaba that Hannah had bought him. He looked everywhere he could think but still could not locate it.

He stood in this place beneath his house. He was here still. The kids were too. Without those objects, that evidence, even without any remaining kindness or comfort or even love, a history would remain.

Their plane had landed at Carthage International, and they had taken a cab to their hotel in Tunis, where they collapsed, exhausted after the wedding and the flight, and slept for hours. When Lovell woke, Hannah was gone. He checked the bathroom and the front lobby, but could not find her. He went back to their room to take a shower, and when he came out, she sat on the bed with several bags of candies that she had bought. "Look, I found this sesame candy, *halwa chamia*. I got some wafers, some candied dates, and these candied chilies."

"You went for a walk without me?" he asked, rubbing the towel through his hair.

"I couldn't just sit here and watch you sleep anymore."

"I thought you were sleeping too."

She shrugged. "I was, for a little while."

They went back out together and wandered around the souks for a while. They stopped at a small café and had chickpea soup and octopus with *harissa* and couscous that had been made with orange-blossom water, and Lovell began to get his energy back. They made love that evening, and they lay in bed afterward, feeding each other candied dates, and admitted to each other being in awe of the fact that they had gotten married and were now on their *honeymoon*.

The next morning she shook him awake. Something was

wrong. "I feel awful," she said. "Like I swallowed a knife or something."

She vomited into the hole in the ground that served as the toilet in their bathroom. He stood behind her, holding her hair back. They wondered whether she had food poisoning. They had been warned not to drink tap water here and had taken the precaution so far of drinking only bottled water, but what about the food? What if some of it had been cooked in tainted water? He thought of the couscous and that orange-blossom water.

Lovell went down to the lobby to ask the location of the nearest pharmacy, but no one was at the front desk. When he returned to the room, he found Hannah on the floor in the bathroom, again vomiting into that filthy hole. He rubbed her back and kissed her head. And she continued to vomit until she passed out.

He splashed water on her face, paced the room, and went down to the lobby again, and again it was empty. Finally she came to and stumbled back to the bed. The next few hours continued on like this until Lovell said, "Come on, come on," and cleaned her up and led her downstairs. He guided her across the street to another hotel and asked the concierge about the nearest hospital. The man told him that an ambulance could take all day, given the traffic in the city. He tried to give Lovell directions to walk there, but his English was only fair and the map in Arabic that he handed over was little help.

Still, Lovell slung one of Hannah's arms over his shoulder

and set off, doing his best to get them headed in the right direction at least. When they passed through the souks, hands grabbed at them. Something slid inside his pocket, and a moment later his wallet was gone. He turned to see who or what had just made off with it, but the crowds were too dense. He pushed his way forward, on past the other souks, and set Hannah down across the sidewalk. She said, "Lovell?" and she looked up at him, maybe afraid for her life.

He said, "I've got you. I've got this," although he was well aware that by now he did not. He lifted her again and carried her to a small restaurant nearby, where someone knew someone else whose cousin was a doctor. "But I have no money," Lovell admitted, and the someone soon disappeared.

At this point, Hannah was draped over a table, her skin white.

Lovell rushed over to the host of the restaurant and told him, "You need to find me a doctor."

The man went to talk to someone else who left and returned with an old man, supposedly a doctor, wearing a white T-shirt and old khakis. He ushered them toward his small car a few blocks away and drove them through the congested city, past the buildings and mosques, over a long bridge, and eventually toward smaller towns and finally past a squat village along a dusty road and into a driveway that led to a tiny stone structure.

He allowed Hannah to rest on a cot that he set up in his cramped basement. He told them he was going out to get medicine and would be back as soon as he could. He gave them a bottle of water and told them that the sounds coming from upstairs, the singing that "sounds like a sick bull"? "That is my wife and she rarely stops. I can do nothing to stop it," he said as he left.

Hannah lay there, looking over at Lovell, blinking fast. "What is going on?" she said.

"I love you."

"I love you too." She closed her eyes. The woman continued to sing in Arabic upstairs. "Am I going to be OK?"

He reached over to touch her forehead. The cot was small, but he edged his way onto the mattress beside her. The basement was dark and smelled awful, like sewage and mold. The woman upstairs sang louder. A truck thundered by outside.

"I am going to die on our honeymoon," she said.

"No, you're not."

"I never should have married you," she said, laughing and coughing at the same time.

"Fuck you."

"Fuck." She could hardly sustain a smile.

"Come here," he said, sitting up now. "Come on. Give me your head," he said, and he moved toward the top of the cot. He slid his hands beneath her head. He bent down and kissed her forehead. He kept his lips there against her damp skin. "We got married," he whispered.

"I'm scared," she said.

"I've got it. Don't be scared."

"What if he doesn't come back?"

"I've got it."

"What if I get sicker?"

"I've got it."

She ran her tongue over her cracked lips. "What if he locked us down here?"

Lovell rose and walked up the stairs to check the door, relieved when the knob turned and the door opened.

"You're the only one that I have right now," she said when he came back.

He nodded.

She looked over at him with something like amazement. "We got married, Love."

"You're my wife now."

"And you're my husband. My *husband*."

Acknowledgments

My thanks to those whose helped me in writing this book: Chris Castellani, Carolyn Cooke, Bret Anthony Johnston, Michael Lowenthal, Ladette Randolph, Jane Roper, Anna Solomon. For assistance with research, thanks to David Linsky and Kate MacDougall. To my team at Algonquin: Emma Boyer, Brunson Hoole, Rachel Careau, Lauren Moseley, Craig Popelars, Elisabeth Scharlatt, and Ina Stern. Thank you to Kathy Pories, talented editor whose keen vision and guidance helped transform this book into what it was meant to be; to Bill Clegg, longtime and invaluable friend, reader, advocate, therapist. Thank you to my sister, Margot Geffen, warm and safe haven. Thank you to my daughter, Amelia, intuition and kindness; to my son, Milo, heart and curiosity; and finally and most importantly to my husband, Neil, superhuman patience and support and unfailing optimism.

||||||||||||||||||||||||||||||||||||||||||||||||||||||||||||||||||||||||||||||||||||||||||||||||||||||||||||||

THE DAYLIGHT MARRIAGE

||||||||||||||||||||||||||||||||||||||||||||||||||||||||||||||||||||||||||||||||||||||||||||||||||||||||||||||

A Note from the Author

*

Questions for Discussion

A Note from the Author

It was July 16, 1999. Some friends and I were hefting huge backpacks into the trunks of our cars after a backwoods camping trip in northern New Hampshire. Someone turned on a car radio and we all heard the news: John F. Kennedy Jr. and Carolyn Bessette-Kennedy, as well as her sister, had disappeared in a small plane just off Martha's Vineyard. I hardly knew anything about these three people. As my friends and I drove back toward civilization, more was said over the radio—gravely, and with alarm—although at that point, not much more was known. Something triggered within me. How did I know so little about these people? I had heard John-John's upper-crusty nickname muttered with a derisive lockjaw. I knew a bit about his dabblings in politics and publishing. Everyone knew about the Kennedy curse. But I knew hardly anything about Carolyn or her sister. Every DJ on every radio station was soon talking about the missing Piper Saratoga. What had happened to them? What was their connection with Martha's Vineyard, where I had spent several summers in college working in restaurants? Wasn't Hyannis Port their domain? As the story unfolded—and with it, rumors of marital discontent, John's failing magazine, Carolyn's possible depression—I found myself oddly riveted. Carolyn soon drifted closer to the center of the story, this lovely, apparently shy woman who rocketed to global fame only after she had died.

At the end of 2002, a beautiful, very pregnant married woman named Laci Peterson disappeared. The media lit up.

Poe wrote, "The death then of a beautiful woman is unquestionably the most poetical topic in the world, and equally is it beyond doubt that the lips best suited for such topic are those of a bereaved lover." I set out to write this novel with an interest in this country's—and my own—obsession with the disappearances of beautiful women.

A few months after I started it, a young mother, Rachel Entwistle, and her baby were shot and killed by her British husband in the very small Massachusetts town where my new husband and I had recently moved. I watched the international media swarm in and the town morph into a temporary city of reporters and cameramen and producers and curious onlookers. The Entwistles had lived about two miles from our house, and I began to go for drives past theirs. I took note of the throngs of people and police tape. I tried to catch a glimpse of a family member or neighbor—a hum in my chest, horrified but intrigued. And utterly ashamed of myself. Wasn't I, literary fiction editor and writer, educated woman and news snob, above this desperate gawking?

I began to think that the media, as well as we, its willing viewers and readers, were reveling in a dark fairy tale: Beautiful woman marries charming, handsome man. Something about the man is not as it seems—perhaps his competence, his loyalty, his morality. His hidden flaw causes her downfall, which inevitably leads to his. Is our enthusiasm for this story the ultimate schadenfreude? The perfect are not in fact perfect. Thank God.

The gap between a person's external and internal lives has always intrigued me. When I began this book, I wanted to tunnel my way inside the archetypes of the beautiful victim and the secretive suspect and unearth some possible complexities. I was curious about how interchangeable the roles of aggressor and victim might be within the bounds of a strained marriage. I hoped to imagine the impact of so much external attention and, with it, so many assumptions for both the beautiful woman during her life and the secretive man after her disappearance. I wanted to travel to the extreme of what might happen when a couple's desires go ignored for years in the face of their daily realities. When their blackest thoughts about each other finally burst forth, when they must face their own dark impulses and wishes in the light of day, what then?

Light plays a significant role in this book—the clear light of one pivotal day in the life of a husband and wife; the blinding flash of cameras; the ever-changing view through a skylight above the couple's bed. *The Daylight Marriage* is a study of exposure—an x-ray of two lives, a marriage, and a culture that professes to love one kind of tale but so often embraces a much darker story.

Questions for Discussion

1. Why do you think Lovell and Hannah chose the jobs that they did? How do their jobs contribute to their fates?

2. The author chose to tell this story from two points of view. What did this narrative choice add to the story?

3. Why do you think Lovell and Hannah ended up getting married and staying together, even after their incompatibilities became clear to them?

4. How does Lovell's work serve as a metaphor for what happens elsewhere in his life?

5. Do you think Hannah's fate was wholly accidental, or did she have some small say in it? Do you think she was entirely unaware of the danger she faced on the beach?

6. What role do the neighbors, Stephen and Jeff, play in this book? Without them, what would be lost?

7. What does the title mean to you?

8. Is Lovell a reliable character? Why or why not?

9. How does the author build suspense in this novel?

10. What does danger mean to Hannah? Why was it necessary to her?

11. Why wasn't Lovell more receptive to the therapist, Dr. Valmer? Why weren't the kids?

12. The members of the Hall family often chide each other for their language. What roles do language and swearing have in this book?

13. What does Janine think has happened to her mother? How does this change throughout the book? Why?

14. Do you think the author wrote this book more as a character study and a literary novel or as a cautionary tale? Why?

15. Hannah once asked Lovell, "Do you ever get sick of trying to predict the precise movement of every molecule in the atmosphere? When you look so close at something, doesn't it start to disappear? Doesn't it lose its fundamental it-ness?" (page 184). What does this mean to you? What do you think Hannah was talking about, beyond Lovell's work?

AYNSLEY FLOYD

Heidi Pitlor is the author of *The Birthdays,* of which Fred Leebron wrote, "Undeniably gratifying . . . Subtly riveting . . . This isn't just a terrific family novel; it's a terrific novel through and through." Formerly a senior editor at Houghton Mifflin, Pitlor is the annual series editor for *The Best American Short Stories.* She lives with her husband and their twins outside Boston.

Other Algonquin Readers Round Table Novels

The Storied Life of A. J. Fikry, a novel by Gabrielle Zevin

A. J. Fikry's life is not at all what he expected it to be. He lives alone, his bookstore is experiencing the worst sales in its history, and now his prized possession, a rare collection of Poe poems, has been stolen. But when a mysterious package appears at the bookstore, its unexpected arrival gives Fikry the chance to see everything anew.

"Engaging and funny . . . Marvelously optimistic about the future of books and bookstores and the people who love both." —*The Washington Post*

"A reader's paradise of the first order." —*The Buffalo News*

AN ALGONQUIN READERS ROUND TABLE EDITION WITH READING GROUP GUIDE AND OTHER SPECIAL FEATURES • FICTION • ISBN 978-1-61620-451-8 • E-BOOK ISBN 978-1-61620-394-8

Descent, a novel by Tim Johnston

The Rocky Mountains have cast their spell over the Courtlands, but when daughter Caitlin and younger brother Sean go out for an early morning run and only one of them comes back, the mountains become as terrifying as they are majestic. Written with a precision that captures every emotion, every moment of fear, this gripping novel races like an avalanche to its heart-pounding conclusion.

"A riveting literary thriller of the can't-stop-turning-the-page, stay-up-all-night variety." —Alice LaPlante, author of *A Circle of Wives*

"Read this astonishing novel . . . The magic of his prose equals the horror of Johnston's story." —*The Washington Post*

AN ALGONQUIN READERS ROUND TABLE EDITION WITH READING GROUP GUIDE AND OTHER SPECIAL FEATURES • FICTION • ISBN 978-1-61620-477-8 • E-BOOK ISBN 978-1-61620-430-3

Pictures of You, a novel by Caroline Leavitt

Two women running away from their marriages collide on a foggy highway. The survivor of the fatal accident is left to pick up the pieces not only of her own life but of the lives of the devastated husband and fragile son that the other woman left behind. As these three lives intersect, the book asks, How well do we really know those we love, and how do we open our hearts to forgive the unforgivable?

"An expert storyteller . . . Leavitt teases suspense out of the greatest mystery of all—the workings of the human heart." —*Booklist*

"Magically written, heartbreakingly honest . . . Caroline Leavitt is one of those fabulous, incisive writers you read and then ask yourself, Where has she been all my life?" —Jodi Picoult

AN ALGONQUIN READERS ROUND TABLE EDITION WITH READING GROUP GUIDE AND OTHER SPECIAL FEATURES • FICTION • ISBN 978-1-56512-631-2 • E-BOOK ISBN 978-1-61620-032-9